TWENTY-SEVEN

SHAYNE WOODSMITH

Cover illustrated by Christian Whitty

SHAYNE WOODSMITH writes, makes movies, and takes photos. His second novel, *My Brother Mercy*, is a deeply personal, heartbreaking, and at times hilarious take on the monotony of daily life, the complexities of familial relationships, and the pursuit of meaning in the seemingly endless loop of day-to-day existence. *My Brother Mercy* was a 2015 Next Generation Indie Book Awards winner.

He is currently working on a collection of short stories and collaborating on a graphic novel. He spends a lot of time compiling the stories and portraits of the inhabitants of Edmonton, Alberta, Canada with his Faces of Edmonton project, which is now a book.

He lives in Edmonton with his spouse Megan and their two cats, Mortimer and Tuna.

Special thanks to Thomas Wharton and M.G. Vassanji for the deadlines and for pushing me to be a better writer.

For Megan.

And thanks mum and dad for not stopping at four children even though you probably wanted to.

PART ONE

ONE

The long bleach-white corridor in the maternity ward had the faintest antiseptic smell, which the nurses and doctors didn't seem to notice anymore. The doctors walked slowly, heads tilted down towards their electronic charts in their hands as they scribbled notes and read through patient histories. The nurses hustled past the doctors from one room to the next, their shoes squeaking against the sterile floor.

Inside one of the nurseries, while the parents watched from behind a gigantic glass wall that separated the nursery from the parent observation lounge, five nurses spread out amongst the twenty perfectly aligned incubators. Hyperventilated cries filled the room, and the newborns shook with the effort, their chubby arms and legs trembling as they wailed. On the right wrist of every baby, an obsidian-coloured thanatometer was fastened—like thick wristwatches with dead batteries. The skin beside the straps was inflamed.

The nurses' thanatometers displayed vital signs, age, and projected death age (PDA). Blood pressure, heart rate, respiratory rate, and body temperature were displayed at the bottom and fluctuated slightly depending on a nurse's level of exertion, but her age and **PDA**, the two largest numbers at the top of the screens, remained fixed. The baby thanatometers would display the same data after calibration but first they needed to be synchronized with the hospital's computer network.

The nurses went from incubator to incubator with styluses in hand, lifting wrists, examining thanatometers, and making the babies bawl louder. After a few strokes of the stylus on a baby thanatometer's glass face, the instrument would connect and begin to glow neon blue.

The parents—some sitting on couches and others standing in the tiered observation lounge—anxiously sipped water from metal tumblers while watching baby names pop up on the glass screen in front of them, obscuring their view of the nursery. Each time a thanatometer began to glow on a baby's wrist, its owner's name would appear on the screen. The parents stared at each new name.

Breyton, Stephanie – PDA 00.00.

Lam, James – PDA 00.00.

Vargez, Carmen – PDA 00.00.

As the gigantic screen filled with baby names, some of the parents began shifting in their seats, others paced the floor, one couple gawked from their seats with their jaws hanging open. Mr. and Mrs. Vargez held their breath for a split second when their daughter's name appeared, dreading the imminent calibration even though they knew there was nothing to worry about. *But what if … what if …*

Mr. Lam stood up. "All right. Here we go," he said as his son's name appeared in front of him. "Let's see those high triple digits." He finished his water with a gulp, put his glass in his chair's cup holder, licked his lips, and began wringing his hands with his gaze fixed on the zeros beside his son's name.

Mrs. Lam rose from her chair, wrapped her arms around her husband's waist, and interlaced her fingers.

"What do you think?" she asked.

"Like his dad." Mr. Lam smirked but didn't take his eyes off the screen. "One hundred and twenty-eight."

"Hey Lam," Mr. Breyton called out from the other side of the room, a cocky smile creeping across his face as he spoke. "Bet you a full day's wage my daughter beats your son by at least five years."

Lam faced him and said, "I'll take that."

"Easy money. Easy money," Breyton said, his eyes shifting back and forth between the poised zeros of James Lam and his little Stephanie.

Mrs. Lam let go of her husband. "Oh dear, please don't," she said and began cracking her knuckles. "We have more important things to worry about."

He turned towards his wife and covered her hands with his, the cracking stopped. "I hope James doesn't fret like his mother," he said. "He might only make it to eighty."

Embarrassed, she dropped her hands to her sides. "Sorry dear, I just ..."

"Don't worry about the bet," he said, smirking at Breyton before turning back to the screen. "It's a lock."

Sean and Lizette Nolan sat directly in front of the large glass screen waiting for their daughter's name to appear. They leaned back, holding hands and staring up. The previous night was the first time the couple had slept apart in years, and Sean had tossed worse than ever. Lying alone in their bed, all he could think of was Sophia's PDA calibration. One second the numbers would soar in his imagination and the next they'd plummet. He had to get up and work out just to distract himself. The treadmill for an hour, weights for an hour and a half, and then thirty minutes of crunches. He'd punished himself like he used to in college the night before a basketball game, especially a playoff game. But it didn't help. Unlike Lizette, he

4

hadn't slept at all. She spent the night in a recovery chamber at the hospital and had had the deepest sleep of her life. At first she didn't think she'd be able to relax. She hated baths and couldn't stand the feeling of shriveled fingers and toes afterwards. But the warm, regenerative plasma she soaked in gave her the wonderful sense of weightlessness. She didn't dream or wake prematurely, and her digits didn't even get pruney. Lizette had surrendered to relaxation completely and was sure it would add years to her life. She had awoken refreshed, her body showing no signs that she was ever pregnant.

Finally Sophia's numbers popped up on the screen.

Nolan, Sophia – PDA 00.00.

The Nolans' eyes widen when they saw their daughter's name and, seemingly pulled towards the screen, they leaned forward and then stood up. Midway through their first date ten years ago, they knew they'd have healthy babies with long lives. They were both extremely fit. He ran marathons and had played competitive basketball since middle school, and she'd been swimming one hundred laps everyday since her sixteenth birthday. Good genes too—no history of any abnormalities on either side. It was a logical certainty that their children would be healthier or at least just as healthy. That thought carried them from their first date to their vows a year later. But now, waiting to confirm what they had always presumed, part of them didn't want to know.

Sean couldn't stop thinking about the saying, "A child's PDA is a parent's life," and Lizette kept hearing her mother's voice saying, "A healthy child is a healthy marriage," over and over. As they waited for Sophia's numbers to move, they both felt as if the memory of their first date wasn't real and that the people they were ten years ago didn't exist, which made them question if they existed at all. They stood still, shoulders close but not touching, holding hands, the feeling of the other's palm completely void of the spark that was there the first time they had touched. Having a child was supposed to bring them closer together, but instead they were each standing beside and holding hands with a stranger.

The nurses filed out of the nursery when all twenty thanatometers glowed and all twenty baby names, ten boys and ten girls, were displayed in rows across the screen in front of the twenty couples. The calibration was about to begin. The parents became very still, their own thanatometers monitoring their elevated heart rates and blood pressures; numbers fluctuated in time with heartbeats, moving up and up as the moment dragged on. And then, the numbers sprang to life.

The PDAs began to increase, soaring through the lower digits, racing upwards like stopwatches in fast forward.

"Come on baby. Come on baby," Mr. Breyton said, his hands clenched into tight fists.

"Oh Stephie. Come on Steph," Mrs. Breyton said through hands cupped over her nose and mouth.

Mr. Lam clapped and said, "Let's go James. Don't let me down."

The numbers began to slow after reaching eighty but continued to move up steadily.

90 ... 93 ... 96 ... 97 ... 100 ...

The pace of each readout steadily slowed down until, nearing one hundred and twenty, the numbers crawled, reaching for the higher digits, exhausted but resolute. Some readings were higher than others now, and the parents of the more ambitious PDAs cheered their children on.

"You can do it. Come on. You can do it."

At one hundred and twenty-two point one five, Stephanie Breyton's digital readout turned black and started pulsating like a steady heartbeat. The Breytons hugged each other and looked down at the digital displays on their own wrists: hers, 121.43, his, 124.91. Steph was, as they had feared, between them but closer to her mother.

"Not bad. Not bad," he said.

"At least she's over one twenty," she said. "That's all I wanted."

One by one the numbers beside the names stopped, turned black, and began flashing on the screen in front of the parents.

127.26.

130.92.

124.48.

129.51.

The room grew evermore boisterous with the pulsating of each PDA. Couples hugged and kissed and high-fived.

"You owe me some money Breyton," Lam said, holding up his glass of water and chuckling.

Breyton nodded, and raised his glass. He was among the minority of more subdued parents who tried to remain phlegmatic while digesting the weaker longevities of their children.

"It's okay. Steph's still above average."

"Don't worry. We'll help her bring that up a bit."

Amidst the celebrations and hard swallows, one PDA hadn't calibrated at all and one couple hadn't moved. The zeros beside Sophia Nolan's name stared back at her parents like gigantic tombstones.

"What happened? What's the matter with it?" Lizette asked.

"I don't know," Sean replied. "It must be a … a glitch or something." He turned to the Lams who were embracing each other beside them. "Hey. Hey!"

They turned, their huge smiles fading when they saw Sean and Lizette's stricken faces.

"Have you ever seen that before?" Sean pointed to his daughter's motionless digits.

The Lams turned to face the screen again. "That's weird," Mr. Lam said. "Hey everybody. Everybody. Excuse me!" The commotion settled as all eyes turned towards Mr. Lam. "Keep it down for a second. One PDA still needs to be calibrated."

Everyone stared at the frozen zeros beside Sophia's name. *Did she have a heartbeat? Was she dead?*

Then her numbers lurched upward and a communal sigh filled the room.

"There we go."

"That's more like it."

Sean and Lizette sighed as they wrapped their arms around each other and collapsed into the chairs behind them.

"Oh thank God," Lizette said.

Mr. Lam leaned in. "It probably stalled 'cause it's going to be so high." He patted Sean on the shoulder. "Huh."

The thought infected the Nolans. Suddenly, the numbers had paused because they were going to be the exclamation point for the entire calibration procedure. As Sophia's numbers increased in a blur, her parents' eyes grew wide at the thought of their daughter breaking the record, about the interviews and the exposés and the magazine cover stories; Lizette imagined herself holding little Sophia while her husband embraced her from behind on the covers; Sean imagined a picture with his daughter in one arm and his wife in the other for their autobiography.

But then both Sophia's counter and time stopped.

Nolan, Sophia – **PDA** 27.00.

The observation lounge became cold and silent. Sean stared at the number. His mouth fell open and he let out an awkward laugh, causing his wife to jerk as if waking from a nightmare and forcing everybody in the room to momentarily turn their eyes from the dead digits to his red face and forced half smile. Sean stood up and stepped forward towards the glass. But just as he got close enough to touch it, just as he extended his arm and reached for the stalled digits, the numbers turned black and began pulsating in sync with all the others on the huge screen. Sean stumbled backwards and crashed down onto the steps.

"We need a doctor in here," Lizette called out, running forward and grabbing hold of Sean beneath his armpits. She tried to lift him but he was dead weight. "Somebody's got to fix that display. There's a loose connection or something … a … a malfunction." Her eyes darted around the room. Everybody, inching closer to their partner, shrank away from the Nolans. Lizette let go of her husband and ran up the stairs towards the back of the room. When she reached the back, she thrust her hand in front of the intercom and waved violently into the motion censor.

"Hello?" she said, her voice raspy. She cleared her throat. "Hello? Hello?"

"Mrs. Nolan?" a crisp voice responded.

"Yes. Yes."

"We're just looking into the problem Mrs. Nolan. We'll run the calibration again when we've finalized all the other PDAs."

Mrs. Nolan edged closer to the intercom, nodded, and said, "Okay."

Mr. Nolan appeared beside her. "No, it's not okay," he said. "Your faulty computer has taken years off our lives, so the next time you run it, you better get it right."

"There's nothing to worry about Mr. Nolan. Occasionally these things happen. Just be patient. We will recalibrate Sophia's PDA soon. It shouldn't be more than a couple of minutes."

"Well, all right," Sean said, running his sweaty palm down the length of his shirt, trying to iron out the wrinkles.

"I will also ask," the voice continued, "that everyone, excluding Mr. and Mrs. Nolan, leave the observing room in an orderly and calm fashion. There has been a slight malfunction with their daughter's thanatometer. All the other calibrations, however, were completed without complications. There is no reason for concern, so kindly make your way towards the exit please."

As soon as the door slid shut behind the last person and the Nolans were alone in the room, the intercom clicked on again. "We are going to restart the calibration. Sophia's numbers will go back down to zero in order for us to do this, so don't be alarmed. It's all part of the procedure."

Sean and Lizette stared at the giant glass wall in front of them—twenty names all paired with numbers were listed in three columns across the screen, every number, except Sophia's, was over one hundred and twenty.

When her readout fell to zero, reset like a primitive watch, both of her parents felt their stomachs drop. They had to sit.

"We're going to restart the calibration. Sorry for the inconvenience."

The digits beside Sophia's name began to roll again. To Lizette, her daughter's name looked out of place on the screen, which made Sophia herself look out of place in the nursery even though she was identical to all the other babies around her.

The numbers increased rapidly but again stopped dead at exactly twenty-seven without any fluctuation.

"Oh my God. What's wrong with her?" Lizette said. "What's wrong with our baby?"

"Nothing's wrong with her," Sean said. "It's just a malfunction. That's all." Sean held his wife tight, trying to push doubt out of his mind.

"There must be something wrong with the wireless connection," the voice said from the intercom. "A nurse will check Sophia's thanatometer momentarily. But until we have confirmation of a proper connection, we will run a full diagnostic of our equipment and then a diagnostic of the connection between Sophia's thanatometer and our system."

"What's the holdup?" Sean called back over his shoulder. "What's wrong with your system?"

"Does this sort of thing happen a lot?" Lizette asked, her head pressed against Sean's chest.

"No." The voice responded. "This sort of thing rarely happens. But rest assured that we will correct the problem."

A nurse entered the nursery on the other side of the screen and quickly made her way to Sophia. After a few strokes of her stylus across Sophia's little thanatometer display, the phosphorescence was extinguished and Sophia's name disappeared from the screen. Then the entire screen went blank. The nurse pulled up a cable from the floor next to the incubator and clicked it into Sophia's thanatometer. When Sophia's thanatometer began to glow once again, her name reappeared on the glass wall, all alone and in the centre. PDA zeroed.

"This time we are using a direct connection to ensure that there is no interference to Sophia's calibration. You will be seeing the most accurate readout possible, down to a thousandth of a year. It'll begin shortly."

Sophia slept. Many of the other babies were fussing and wailing, but Sophia didn't seem to hear them.

The nurse examined Sophia, the incubator, and the connection between Sophia's thanatometer and the cable before leaving the nursery and entering the observation lounge.

"Hello," she said, approaching the Nolans. "Is there anything I can get for either of you?"

"You could get these damned machines to do their jobs and you could do yours too while you're at it."

"Sean," Lizette said, glaring at her husband.

The nurse cleared her throat. "Can I get you anything ma'am?"

"Ice water please," she said.

"Of course. I'll be right back with it."

After the nurse left, the room was silent. Lizette's ears were ringing.

"What does this mean, Sean?"

He turned to her. "It doesn't mean anything."

"But what if …" She swallowed and tried to moisten her dry throat. "What if that's her PDA? What if …"

"It's not." He turned to look at Sophia's name on of the screen. "It can't be. It's just a ridiculous malfunction."

Lizette gazed through the glass at the cable connecting her daughter to the floor. She reached towards Sophia, her baby who suddenly seemed small and sickly. Her reddened skin and rapid breaths couldn't be healthy. Lizette stretched out her hand but let it fall to her side when the nurse stepped through the door with two glasses of ice water.

"Thanks," Lizette said.

After handing over the glasses, the nurse moved to the back of the room and stood by the intercom. The intercom broke the silence.

"We're going to recalibrate now."

"It's about time!" said Sean.

"Once again, I apologize for the long wait and the technical problems. Your daughter's PDA will, normal and ample, appear momentarily … here we go."

The Nolans and the nurse fixed their eyes on the numbers poised to increase in the centre of the glass wall. Once Sophia's PDA began to increase for the third time, it was a slow methodical climb, digit by digit and tenth of a year by tenth of a year until the counter, again, stopped at twenty-seven.

The nurse's entire body went limp. She shook her head thinking that somehow a one would appear in front of the poor child's feeble projected death age.

"What does that mean?" Lizette asked. She turned back to the nurse, her voice shaky, her hand gripping the back of her seat. "What do we do now?"

"We don't do anything now," Sean said. "They've got to fix the computers or else we'll never know Sophia's real PDA."

"What does that mean?" Lizette cried out, forcing the nurse to look at her.

"It doesn't mean anything," Sean said.

Lizette jumped to her feet, marched up to the nurse, and grabbed both her hands. "Tell me. Please." She squeezed harder. "What does it mean?"

"It … it means what it always means," the nurse said.

"But. It can't. Twenty-seven." Her eyes welled up and her lower lip quivered. "It's … it's so young." Lizette's face fell into her hands and her sobs began to echo throughout the large, empty room.

The nurse wrapped her arm around Lizette's trembling back. "I'm sorry," she said. "I'm so sorry."

TWO

Inside the thanatometer calibration lab, four doctors stood huddled around a large computer screen, abandoning the nine other screens inside the room. At the top of the screen that mesmerized the doctors, all of Sophia's vital signs—her age, blood pressure, heart rate, respiratory rate, body mass index, and organ function —were listed beneath her name. In the centre of the screen was Sophia's mapped genome, all twenty-three chromosome pairs lined up beside each other in parallel columns. And at the bottom of the screen, where the doctors stared, transfixed, was the number twenty-seven beside three capital letters: PDA.

"How can this be?" asked Dr. Benoit, tucking her long, auburn hair behind her ears and crossing her arms. "I've never seen anything like this."

Dr. Zoller squinted at the digits and said, "That's because nothing like this has ever happened before."

"This is astounding," Dr. Nanako said, waving her hands around in front of herself as she spoke. "The lowest PDA in, in … at least a century."

"The lowest PDA ever," Dr. Zoller replied.

Dr. Watts, without saying anything, leaned forward with his right hand outstretched and tapped on the screen with the nail of his index finger, rapping on the numbers as if to wake them. When the digits wouldn't budge, he eased himself down into a chair and sighed.

The door to the lab opened, and Rubin Russell stepped inside. The doctors turned towards him. Rubin felt surprisingly relieved to be there even after seeing the four stricken faces. Not even the worst urgent situation could be bad enough to make him want to be back in that boardroom.

Before entering the calibration lab, Rubin sat at the end of a long table listening to Tabitha Spencer, the CEO of the National Wellness, pontificate about the superior direction National Wellness has taken since she stepped in. He knew nothing had changed in decades. All Tabitha had done, and all she ever did—other than signing off on the work of others—was shuffle around some numbers. She lived for those meetings because preparing for them was the only real work she ever did.

Rubin had already been in the department heads meeting for an hour when a secretary snuck inside the boardroom without knocking. She approached him, bent down, and whispered, "Sorry to interrupt Mr. Russell but they need you in the calibration lab. A newborn's PDA stopped abruptly."

Tabitha didn't seem to notice the intrusion and continued droning on about the technological and physiological synergy that is longevity: "We must continue to fund and support this prefect marriage. Which is why I'm proposing a funding increase for research and development. The amount of capital put towards R and D is directly proportional to the median PDA. Which brings me to my next point."

At that moment, the secretary slinked out of the boardroom. Rubin sat perfectly still, staring down at a scratch on the thick bamboo table in front of him, the secretary's words ringing in his ears. *Abruptly stopped. Abruptly stopped.* He had to get downstairs. Thinking he could slip out of the meeting unnoticed, Rubin stood up slowly.

"Something the matter, Rubin?" Tabitha said, breaking off from her speech.

The seven other department heads turned to him. Everyone looked the same with their grey business suits and expectant eyes. Except Sasha, the chief nurse executive, who always wore her happy baby blue scrubs to go with her constant smile.

Rubin, moving more quickly now that all eyes were on him, pushed in his chair and stepped towards the door.

"Sorry, I didn't want to interrupt. I'm needed downstairs," he said, straightening his tie.

"Can't it wait?" Tabitha asked. "The meeting has barely begun."

If you have barely begun speaking, Rubin thought, *then leaving can't wait.*

"Sorry. It's urgent."

He opened the door and tried to step out before Tabitha could say anything else, but he wasn't quick enough.

"Well, what is it?"

He turned back, everyone still looking at him. Sasha sat closest to him, her eyes wider than the others. Rubin almost laughed when he noticed her expression; it said, "Take me with you. Please!" After making eye contact with Tabitha, he concentrated on the soothing blue of Sasha's scrubs to maintain his composure.

"A thanatometer has malfunctioned during calibration," he said.

"Malfunctioned? In what way," Tabitha asked.

Rubin hesitated but then said, "It, stopped abruptly."

"Perhaps it wasn't finished calibrating," Tabitha said. "What did it stop at?"

"I'm not sure," he replied. "I was just told that my presence was urgently required."

"Fine, fine," Tabitha said, waving her hand at Rubin. "Just try to make it back before the end of the meeting." She turned her gaze back to the others at the table. "Now, as I was saying…"

Rubin left the boardroom and made his way down the hall. He could still hear Tabitha's voice when he stepped into the elevator and said, "Second floor."

The doctors stopped talking when they saw Rubin, the chief operating officer of National Wellness. He met all their eyes in turn, his short, black hair combed back, his tailored suit hugging his wiry frame. With his hands behind his back, he traipsed around the room examining the three-dimensional images displayed on the nine different workstation screens. Each screen was dedicated to a particular anatomical system. Rubin briefly studied each image of Sophia's different systems in turn while the doctors waited for him to speak. Rubin then approached the screen in the middle of the room that the doctors were gathered around. The doctors stepped aside, making room for him to get through. Rubin saw Sophia's PDA then looked to Dr. Watts.

"So?"

Dr. Watts continued to stare at the screen speechlessly.

Rubin turned to the other doctors. "What can you tell me?"

"It's inexplicable," said Dr. Nanako.

"We've never seen a PDA so low," Dr. Zoller said.

"There's never been one so low," said Dr. Benoit.

"Wait a second," Rubin said, raising his hand to silence them. "I was under the impression that this." He gestured to Sophia's PDA. "Was a malfunction. That something went haywire in the system."

"It's not a malfunction," said Dr. Zoller. "The system is working perfectly."

"Really?" Rubin said, staring at the number twenty-seven and glancing at the empty space in front of the number where a one should have been. "Could the thanatometer have a faulty display?" He leaned closer to the screen. "Perhaps it's just not displaying the one that is in fact preceding these numbers."

"The thanatometer is functioning properly," said Dr. Nanako. "We've made sure of that."

Rubin didn't speak for a moment.

Dr. Zoller stepped closer to Rubin and said, "What we're trying to tell you is that this is an exceptional irregularity."

"But it's not set in stone. Right?" Rubin said. He raised his eyebrows. "It doesn't necessarily mean she can't live longer. Does it?"

Dr. Nanako pointed at the digits, as if Rubin hadn't seen them, and said, "It means what it says—twenty-seven years."

Rubin started to pace. He thought about the child's parents, how devastated they must feel. Then he thought of Tabitha and wrapped a hand around the base of his skull. He'd have to tell her no matter how much he didn't want to. Rubin began massaging his neck. He could see the headlines, imagine the extensive investigation, and almost feel Tabitha reprimanding him as if it were somehow his fault.

"But perhaps," he began, "she'll be able to increase it later on with a regimented lifestyle. Most people can and do."

"And perhaps she won't be able to," Dr. Benoit said, shaking her head and appearing apologetic.

Dr. Nanako kept pointing at the digits. "And what would she increase it to anyway? Thirty? Forty?"

Dr. Zoller placed his hand on Dr. Nanako's shoulder to calm her and addressed Rubin. "It didn't fluctuate," he said. "Every PDA fluctuates a little during calibration, but hers didn't. All PDAs move up and down throughout one's life depending on how one lives, hers should be no different."

"The computers are infallible," Dr. Watts finally said, still staring at the screen. Everyone turned to look down at him. Gesturing to Sophia's genome, he said, "Based on her physiology and barring accidental death, that's how long she'll live."

"Can it be wrong?" Rubin asked.

None of the doctors answered.

"Can her thanatometer, her read out, her PDA be wrong?"

"No," replied Dr. Watts.

"Thanatometers don't predict the future," said Dr. Zoller. "Their function is based on organismal and cellular senescence."

"So are you telling me that this baby will die of old age at twenty-seven?" Rubin asked, his expression skeptical as he looked around at all the doctors. "Are you actually saying that?"

"Yes," said Dr. Zoller. "Well, maybe not of old age but at twenty-seven she'll die of molecular damage that will cause a lack of homeostasis within her body. It's the same thing all thanatometer accurately determine."

"However," Dr Benoit began, "I am not sure how such molecular damage resulting in death could occur at such a young age."

"Could it be a disease? A virus of some kind?" Rubin asked, staring at Sophia's readout. "Does she need to be quarantined?"

"Impossible," cried Dr. Nanako. "Everything checks out. She is perfectly healthy. Identical to any other baby in that room."

"There hasn't been a death do to a virus or a disease in, in …"

"In over fifty years. And besides we would have found it during calibration."

"Absolutely. Nothing can escape detection from our system once we're synchronized with a thanatometer. We can literally see right through a person. We see everything."

"Everything except why her PDA is so low," Rubin said.

The doctors paused for a moment as if offended.

"So what does this mean?" Rubin continued. "Will she die twenty-seven years from today? Is this her projected death age?" Rubin looked around the room at all the uncertain faces surrounding him. "Well?"

"That's her PDA," said Dr. Watts.

"You sure?"

All four doctors nodded while looking around at each other.

"Fine." Rubin moved towards the door. It slid open. "Run every test again. I wanna be sure of her PDA and that she's not communicable," he said. "And give her a new thanatometer. I know that one is probably fine but we have to be sure."

He left the calibration lab before the doctors could protest and marched down the hall towards the parents' observation lounge. Inside, a nurse tidied the dirty glasses left behind by the parents.

Rubin looked around the empty room and said, "Where'd the Nolans go?"

The nurse turned to see him standing in the doorway. "They've gone home for the day sir but they'll be back tomorrow to pick up their baby along with everybody else," she said with glasses in her hands, moving towards the back corner of the room.

"How were they?"

"Distraught," she said, putting down the glasses and looking at Rubin.

He nodded and turned to leave when she called out, "What's wrong with her?"

With one foot in the doorway and the other in the outside hall, Rubin regarded the nurse without responding.

"The baby I mean. Does she have … I mean is there anything …"

"Nothing's wrong with her, okay," Rubin said.

The nurse nodded, and Rubin left the room.

He marched down the hall again. After passing the nursery door, his pace slowed until he stopped in the middle of the hallway. Rubin glanced back at the entrance to the nursery then took another few steps before stopping again. He stood still for a moment wondering what Sophia looked like. He was sure he'd be able to pick her out right away, a sickly little thing closer to death on her first day of life than he was at fifty-five. He still wanted to see her though. But Sophia was a case. Soon to be a case number. He didn't need to see her. He just wanted to.

Rubin spun around and walked into the nursery. He paused and examined the room before strolling around its perimeter. All the babies closest to the walls seemed normal enough, crying, fussing, gurgling, kicking their stubby little legs inside of their jumpsuits. Rubin moved deeper into the room and looked down at every thanatometer on each and every wrist, but all were normal. As he worked his way inward, the babies became less and less fussy, moving from wails to sobs to moans to silent explorations of their surroundings. Still, none of them were Sophia and not one baby looked unhealthy. Rubin approached a group of sleeping babies and saw Sophia right away. He knew it was her. He sensed it. Rubin looked at the thanatometer to make sure. Sophia, and all the other babies directly around her, slept. She was a beautiful, healthy girl. Only her thanatometer readout made her appear weak.

Rubin watched her, lying on her back, clothed in white, her left arm stretched above her head, the other limp at her side, her eyes moving rapidly under her eyelids, her soft, almost translucent hair appearing to float above her tiny head without being attached. She wasn't red-faced from constantly screaming or frail as he had imagined. She was strong and completely calm. Not a single worry.

He reached out and touched Sophia's miniature palm with his index finger. When he did, she grabbed hold of his finger and smiled. Rubin gazed down at her little grin and his shoulders released and his breathing slowed and deepened and his forehead relaxed and the muscles behind his ears—the muscles he didn't even realize were flexed—loosened up, dropping his ears and closing his eyes. In the palm of Sophia's hand the floor liquefied and gravity vanished and all the other cries disappeared. Rubin hovered there, stuck somewhere between sinking down and floating up, until Sophia let go.

When she let go, Rubin opened his eyes and thought of Tabitha. He knew he had to tell her everything right away but he didn't want to. If she saw Sophia as a threat to her legacy, and she would, Tabitha was liable to do anything from ordering a quarantine to demanding the most intrusive examinations of Sophia's anatomy be preformed.

Rubin didn't want to leave Sophia's side. As long as he was with her, she was safe. Safe from Tabitha and anyone else who would cut her open if it meant finding an answer to how a person could die of old age at twenty-seven.

THREE

Death at 27

Nearly two centuries ago, Eli Finn passed away at the age of ninety-eight, immortalizing him as the last person to die of old age before his one-hundredth birthday. Since Eli's death, projected death ages have exceeded one hundred years without exception—until last Friday when a child was born with the youngest PDA ever recorded: twenty-seven.

This child, known only as "baby Sophia," is currently under quarantine and at the centre of an extensive National Wellness investigation. The investigation, however, has failed to illuminate any possible explanation for the child's unnaturally low PDA.

"She is a normal, healthy baby," said one hospital staff member who chose to remain anonymous. "There are no abnormalities in any of her anatomical systems, her DNA and genome are sound, and there are, of course, absolutely no pathogens present in any part of her body. The quarantine is merely a temporary, precautionary measure."

Other precautionary measures, such as performing complete diagnostics of computer networks and ramping up security of those networks, are being employed at hospitals around the world. But nobody expects the anomaly within baby Sophia's thanatometer to reoccur.

"This is an isolated incident," said a spokesperson from National Wellness. "It has never happened before and it will never happen again."

When asked about the parents of baby Sophia, the spokesperson said, "They have above average PDAs and conceived their child through lawful, healthy, and natural means."

Asked if baby Sophia's inexplicable condition will encourage doctors to recommend extracorporeal pregnancy over traditional pregnancy to couples qualifying for procreation permits, the spokesperson said, "The choice between a traditional pregnancy and a factitious womb is one that all permitted couples have to make and this incident will not change that. Our doctors aren't there to sway couples. They are there to help couples make an informed decision about which pregnancy method best suits their individual situation."

It is uncertain, however, how the lowest PDA on record belonging to a child born of traditional pregnancy will affect the type of pregnancy future parents choose to have.

Also uncertain is whether or not baby Sophia will be able to increase her PDA with the help of a rigorous and strictly controlled lifestyle. As neither the diets nor the exercise routines of baby Sophia's parents are suspected of having lowered her PDA, it is presumed that neither will greatly affect the malleability of her PDA in the future.

However, considering that as of today the maximum increase in any one person's PDA has been ten years and the average is two years, it is highly unlikely that baby Sophia will ever reach her fortieth or perhaps even her thirtieth birthday.

Sitting back in the boardroom in the same seat he had left three hours before, Rubin read the article off a tablet screen. There were two new additions to the table, Assistant Attorney General Amos Shantz and Elizabeth Rosenberger, the Deputy Minister for National Wellness, who both sat on the opposite end of the table from him and quietly waited, as did everyone else, for Rubin to finish reading. Tabitha's tall, extremely thin assistant stood behind him, casting a shadow onto his screen.

When Rubin finished reading, he held the tablet up over his shoulder without looking back; the assistant grabbed it and returned to her boss's side like an obedient pet. Rubin glanced around at the people gawking at him. Other than Sasha, who still wore her baby blue scrubs, Tabitha, and the two newcomers, he couldn't think of anyone's name. They were simply the professional acronyms that followed their names. The CFO sat beside Rubin and the CMO beside him. The DHR, a stocky woman with a wide mouth and bulging eyes, sat next to Sasha. Sasha's expression didn't make Rubin feel like laughing anymore. Instead he felt as if he were about to be reprimanded; it was in her face, concern that bordered on fear. Rubin understood why when he noticed how Assistant Attorney General Shantz and Deputy Minister Rosenberger were regarding him. With their fingers poised over the tablet screens in front of them to record Rubin's every word, they stared at him as if he were responsible for Sophia's PDA and was about to explain how he did it.

Tabitha's assistant, cradling her tablet in one arm, was also ready to take notes. The rest had their fingers interlaced and resting on the table in front of them. Rubin wanted to lean back, put his hands behind his head, and his feet up on the table, soles facing Tabitha. But he couldn't lean back. Couldn't even slouch in those ergonomic chairs.

"Do you know how they found out? Who told them?" Tabitha asked, her tone thick with accusation.

Rubin surveyed the seven faces in front of him and ran his index finger and thumb down the length of his tie. "I don't know," he said, putting his hands in his lap. "Somebody must have leaked it. It could have been anyone. One of the other parents. A nurse. Anyone."

"Well, based on the details in the article, I'm sure it was somebody who works here. Someone well informed," Tabitha said, making eye contact with Shantz. "Fortunately," Tabitha continued, "thanks to our HR department, I was able to make a statement for National Wellness and make the article appear as if we notified the paper ourselves." Tabitha paused to give a nod to the bulgy-eyed stocky woman. This made the woman's large mouth spread across her face in a grin while her broad shoulders shrugged up closer to her ears.

"I informed them of the child's isolation from the other babies," Tabitha continued. "And then immediately ordered the quarantine after I got off the phone." She leaned forward and pointed a finger at Rubin, her eyes widening. "Something you should have done the moment you found out about her." Tabitha blinked slowly and sat up even straighter.

Rubin raised a hand to respond, but Tabitha continued without noticing.

"I believe," Tabitha began, glancing around the room and gesturing to the others, "as many of you have since agreed, that the mention of quarantine in the article will provide comfort for those reading it."

Or cause unnecessary panic, Rubin thought, lowering his hand.

"No one will hear the story again, and her PDA will be quickly forgotten." Tabitha turned her gaze to Rubin. "Do you agree, Rubin?"

Everyone turned towards him. He wanted to disagree out of petulance but he knew she was right.

"People will want to forget about her as fast as possible," Rubin said. "Nobody wants to hear about a baby with such a low PDA."

While believing this to be true for most people, Rubin knew that he would never forget Sophia or her PDA. And neither, he figured, would anyone else in that room. He looked down at his finger and remembered how gigantic it seemed when Sophia wrapped her warm hand around it and smiled. That tiny innocent grin somehow defied the numbers on the thanatometer strapped to her little wrist.

"We've decided," Tabitha said, gesturing to the others at the table, "that another complete physical of this baby, of this Sophia, needs to be done right away. We have to know everything about her. Absolutely everything must be documented for our investigation." She tilted her head down slightly, her eyes turned up to look at Rubin. "Which brings me to you."

"I'll take care of the physical," Rubin said, thinking he could stop them from going too far.

"You will," Tabitha said, "and as Chief Operating Officer, you'll be in charge of monitoring Sophia." A smirk, meant only for Rubin to see, flashed across her face.

Rubin wanted to sneer back at her but refrained.

Then Amos Shantz spoke for the first time. "Keep a detailed report."

Rubin turned towards the AAG. He wanted to forget his name and who he was. His words would have been less meaningful then.

"Talk to her doctors and parents and anyone else who might have pertinent information regarding the child's health."

Rubin would have preferred Tabitha telling him because Shantz's lawyerly tone made Rubin feel as if legal action would be taken against him if he didn't comply.

"Later on," Shantz continued, "you'll want to speak with her teachers and friends. Keep us up to date with any abnormalities or sources of concern. Anything out of the ordinary must be flagged and brought to our attention immediately." Then he began scribbling ferociously on his tablet.

Rubin watched the attorney's moving stylus for a moment before responding. "For how long?" he asked.

"Until she turns twenty-seven, of course," Tabitha said.

For a second Rubin thought he heard her wrong, that she hadn't just given him a twenty-seven-year assignment.

"And longer. If it comes to that," Shantz added without looking up from his tablet.

"Whoa, whoa, whoa," Rubin said, throwing his hands up in front of himself. "Starting when?"

"Today," said the Deputy Minister, her voice void of emotion.

"Today?" Rubin echoed, rubbing his forehead. He felt trapped. The Deputy Minister's orders were practically royal decree for a National Wellness employee. Rubin could almost hear the implied words —or else. He squeezed his temples, twenty-seven years.

"Now Rubin, don't stress to the point where you lose months off your PDA," Tabitha said. "Your current workload will of course be lightened. A few of your duties will be delegated to others in order to make room for your new assignment. Alright?"

Rubin didn't answer right away. He knew he didn't have a choice. His head fell back against the headrest. He pictured Sophia sleeping in her incubator. She was completely at peace, with no idea of what her existence meant or that the whole world was talking about her.

When would she begin to understand what her thanatometer says? How would she change?

Rubin knew her ignorance wouldn't last; Sophia was just a baby. She didn't know any better. But soon she would, and suddenly he was supposed to be there through it all. To witness the full weight of her fleeting existence crash down on her and then document everything in a report.

How will she take it? What will she do? Rubin wondered.

He wanted to help her. Be there for her. First, he had to get her out of quarantine and away from the computers analyzing every aspect of her physiology. He imagined her fussing and crying. He needed to get to her.

"Alright Rubin?" Tabitha asked.

Rubin nodded.

"Great. The focus needs to be on why she's different," Tabitha said. "Why her thanatometer says what it does. But most importantly, we need to know what will happen to her when she turns twenty-seven." Her face brightened slightly. "This report could be the single greatest account of a person's health since the findings published about the first calibrated thanatometer. Perhaps even more significant."

Rubin didn't want to contribute to Tabitha's legacy as National Wellness CEO, but she was right. The potential implications for the medical community were enormous and exciting. So much so that Sophia could be forgotten while everyone tripped over each other to get answers.

"Any questions?" Shantz asked.

"What about the family?" Rubin replied. "How important are they to the report?"

"Very," Shantz said. "Keep in constant contact with the parents. Their lives are almost as important as the child's. No house calls or anything but you should meet at regular intervals. After the child's checkups, if they notice anything unusual, etcetera, etcetera. In fact, you should meet with them tomorrow. Pull their triple P and their pre-conception physicals. We need to rule out the obvious answers first."

"Right. That'll be the first phase of your report," Tabitha said. "So it's vital that you stay in constant contact with the parents but, as for the child, I see no need for you to physically be in her life. Your relationship with her will be through her parents and doctors."

"Right. Maintaining an emotional distance would be best I think," Shantz said. "For the preservation of objectivity."

Rubin suppressed the urge to bring his fist down on the table and yell no. He knew they'd all jump if he did. Instead, he did what they expected: he nodded.

Besides, they were right, an investigation this important required distance from the subject.

"Great," Tabitha said. "Nothing slips through the cracks on this. Okay, Rubin? We want to know absolutely everything. The most minute detail could be the key to understanding the plight of this poor girl."

It was hard for Rubin not to roll his eyes. The strategic furrow in Tabitha's brow didn't fool him. He knew she didn't care about Sophia. Nobody at that table did. They only cared about solving a puzzle and getting the credit. If he hadn't seen Sophia, hadn't touched her, he might have felt the same way.

"Now, if there isn't anything else, I think we should adjourn for the day. We have a lot of work to do," Tabitha said. She turned to her lanky assistant, who bent to speak into her ear.

While everyone readied to leave, Rubin stood up and marched out of the boardroom. He moved quickly down the outer hall, his ears buzzing from the silence of his new surroundings, buzzing from the order he had just been given. He watched the floor move beneath him and rubbed the sandpaper stubble on his cheeks, the smooth, clean feeling of his morning shave a distant memory now. He was sweating, his heart pounding. He glanced down at his thanatometer to see if his PDA had moved, but it held steady at 127.37. Knowing that it hadn't dropped helped calm him.

He thought about Sophia and quickened his pace. Part of him never wanted her twenty-seventh birthday to come, wanted to hold her against his chest and keep her safe. But another part, the part that made him move ever faster down the hall, couldn't wait for that day to be over.

FOUR

Rubin's office was large but only a desk with two chairs facing it and a densely populated bookshelf occupied the space. His office door was open, as it always was when he had a meeting, giving him a perfect view of the corridor leading to his office—he liked to see people approach before they knocked on his door.

While waiting for Mr. and Mrs. Nolan to arrive for their appointment, Rubin sat at his desk in his office scrolling through their file. Both of Sophia's parents were extremely healthy. The physical and thanatometer examinations required for procreation permission permit approval were above average. As such, a PPP was issued without question. They were the ideal candidates to have children. But not anymore. Rubin scrolled down to their PPP; it had 'SUSPENDED' written in large, red letters on an angle across the middle of the document. The word appeared just below the individual pictures of Sean and Lizette Nolan, making the expression-neutral photos look like mug shots. Rubin stared at the permit and couldn't think of how to tell the Nolans that their biological right had just been revoked. When he looked up from his screen, he saw the Nolans hesitantly approaching his open door. Rubin slid his tablet into the middle drawer of his desk and stood up to greet them.

"Please come in," he said, stepping around his desk.

He extended his hand to Lizette as she made her way into the room. Rubin squeezed her hand between both of his and said, "Thank you so much for making the time to see me before you take Sophia home with you today. I know you've had a trying twenty-four hours."

Rubin let go of Lizette's hand and turned to Sean. Sean glanced down at Rubin's extended hand and reluctantly shook it.

"It's nice to meet you both in person. Please," Rubin said, gesturing to the two chairs facing his desk. "Have a seat."

As the Nolans sat down, Rubin closed the door and paused for a moment to look at the backs of his guests. They sat up straight and appeared calm from behind. Rubin briefly contemplated staying behind them for the entire meeting to avoid eye contact and facial expressions. Then he sighed, took his hand off the doorknob, and made his way back to his seat.

He smiled but his guests didn't reciprocate. Their faces were flushed and their eyes red. The mother looked haggard, as if she'd be up all night worrying.

The father just seemed annoyed to be there. Rubin's friendly smile faded. He offered them something to drink and, after they declined, he interlaced his fingers and leaned forward with his forearms on his desk.

"Like I said on the phone. I'm Rubin Russell. The Chief Operating Officer here at National Wellness."

"We know," Sean said. "It says so on your door."

"Right, well." Rubin glanced from Sean to his name and professional acronym etched onto the door. Then he turned his attention to Lizette. "How are you two doing?"

"I don't know," Lizette said. "The whole thing just doesn't seem real."

"Listen, we didn't come here for a therapy session, okay," Sean said, leaning forward.

"Well, that's good because I'm not a psychologist," Rubin replied.

What he wanted to say was, *I'm just doing my job. What I was told. So lay off and lighten up.* What stopped him though, was Sophia. She'd be dead in twenty-seven years, and the man sitting in front of him would have to mourn her death for almost sixty years.

"But I am here to help," Rubin continued. "I understand how hard this must be for you."

"Do you have a child who's going to die before you're sixty?" Sean asked, his fists clenched.

Rubin shook his head. "No, I don't."

"Then don't presume to understand. You don't even understand Sophia's PDA. And isn't *that* supposed to be your area of expertise?"

Lizette shifted in her seat. Rubin kept his attention on Sean.

"Mr. Nolan, your daughter's life expectancy is not the fault of National Wellness and it isn't your fault either. You're here today because we want the same things. We both want what's best for your daughter, we both want to understand why her PDA is so low, and we want Sophia to live a much longer life than is currently projected. Okay? We need to help each other."

"Well, if you care so much about our daughter, why don't you explain to us why——"

"Sean, please don't," Lizette said.

Sean began to talk louder, over his wife's much softer voice. "Why you had that article written up about our family?"

Rubin remained still. He had hoped they wouldn't see the article yet somehow he knew they would.

"I'm sorry you had to read about yourselves like that, Mr. and Mrs. Nolan. But National Wellness didn't instigate that article. We simply responded to it in the best interests of everyone involved."

Sean leaned back again and said, "Maybe you didn't instigate it but somebody working here sure as hell did."

"Unfortunately, some of our employees decided to go against their better judgment and the policies outlined in National Wellness's code of conduct. They spoke without the consent of National Wellness and they will be reprimanded," Rubin said, knowing that the people who spoke to the press would probably never be found out. "They also spoke out without knowing all of the facts."

"So what's the investigation they talked about in the article? Is that what this is? Are you investigating us?" Sean asked.

Rubin stood, walked around his desk, and sat down on it. He faced the Nolans. "In order to get to the bottom of why Sophia's PDA is so low, I've been charged with monitoring her as she grows up."

"Monitoring her?" Lizette said. "What does that mean?"

"It means that we'll be constantly watching her thanatometer readout and recording her vital signs. However, this will be done without inconveniencing you or your daughter in anyway. We will simply establish a permanent connection to her thanatometer so that we will have remote access to Sophia's health at every moment."

"How long will you need to monitor her for," Lizette asked.

"For the rest of her life," Rubin said, staring back at Lizette. The darkness and wrinkles around her eyes seemed to worsen. She appeared almost ten years older than she was, and Rubin assumed that the past twenty-four hours were to blame. He didn't want to take even more years off her life, but she needed to know.

"What about checkups?" Lizette asked. "How often will she need to come in?"

"Screw checkups," Sean said, jerking forward in his seat. "What about her privacy? What about our privacy? This article got published without your knowledge. Who's to say all the data you collect on Sophia won't be as well."

Rubin crossed his arms, looked down at Mr. Nolan, and said, "Your daughter's privacy and your family's privacy is our priority. I will be the only person with complete access to Sophia's information, which will be analyzed by a group of doctors who will report directly to me. That article could have been leaked by one of the other parents or a member of our nursing staff with access to the hospital network …" Rubin's voice trailed off.

"And you've changed that now, right?" Lizette asked.

Rubin smiled at Mrs. Nolan and then walked back around his desk and sat down.

"Not even the Minister of Health could access Sophia's file without my consent. Now." Rubin turned to Sean. "Does that ease your mind Mr. Nolan?"

Sean crossed his arms and said, "A little."

"Fine then. And to answer your question Mrs. Nolan," Rubin continued.

"Lizette."

"Lizette, as for checkups, Sophia will need to see our doctors once a year. And, other than for new thanatometer fittings, you'll only need to bring her in if there is an accident or if we notify you that we'd like to see her. Now, if there is an emergency, Sophia breaks her leg or anything like that, you'll need to bring her here. Taking her to see any other doctor would be out of the question considering her circumstances. On our way down to pickup Sophia, I will introduce you to three of our best doctors. One of them will be tending to Sophia each time she comes in. Do you have any questions so far?"

"So we can never travel," Sean said.

"Of course you can travel. You may go anywhere you like as long as you notify us beforehand so that we know where you are. If something happens, let us know and one of our doctors will meet you at the closest medical facility. Sophia has a right to her doctor, and we can get practically anywhere within a few hours."

Sean stood and walked towards the wall of books beside him.

Rubin watch Sean examine his collection and said, "No government in the world will violate that right."

Sean fingered a few of the book spines and said, "You read all these?"

"Most of them," Rubin said.

Sean meandered back to his chair, sat down, and, after exhaling loudly, said, "You must have a lot of spare time on your hands."

Rubin surveyed the bookshelf. "Some people watch TV," he said, "I read."

"Seems weird to have all that paper just sitting there on a shelf like that. Seems like a fire hazard to me. You don't like your tablet or what?"

"When reading for pleasure, I like to feel the pages between my fingers. But for work," Rubin said, opening the middle drawer of his desk and producing his tablet, "I use this."

"My grandmother has a large book collection as well," Lizette said.

"Does she?" Rubin said, smiling at Lizette.

"She inherited it when her grandmother died and her mother threatened to give the books to a museum."

"Do either of you have any hobbies or collections?" Rubin asked, looking back and forth between them.

"I run," Sean said, his left leg now shaking up and down.

Rubin's first thought was, *Everybody runs*. But he nodded and turned to Lizette.

"I um, I …"

"She collects dead butterflies," Sean said.

Lizette shot a look at Sean and then turned her gaze to the ground.

"Butterflies are very beautiful," Rubin said.

Lizette looked at Rubin. "I have over twenty extinct species," Lizette said, becoming more animated. "I even have a Queen Alexandra's Birdwing. It was the largest known butterfly."

"I'd like to see it sometime," Rubin said.

Lizette smiled. Sean's leg shook more violently.

"Well, I'm sure you're anxious to get home with Sophia, so we should probably finish up," Rubin said. He looked down at his tablet, the suspended PPP of Mr. and Mr. Nolan stared back at him. He closed the document and opened a new one. "I need your signatures on an authorization form," Rubin said, standing and walking towards Sean with his tablet held out.

Sean took the tablet and began reading. Rubin passed him the stylus. Lizette tried to read over her husband's shoulder.

"It states everything that we just talked about," Rubin said. "And acknowledges that you were made aware of the steps National Wellness intends to take to safeguard your privacy and care for your daughter."

"I'm not signing this without a lawyer," Sean said, holding the tablet out to Rubin.

Rubin didn't take the tablet. Instead he sat back on his desk and gripped the hard wood on either side of his legs. "I don't need your permission, Mr. Nolan," Rubin said, his voice turning cold. "This is a courtesy. If

I'm going to be in your lives for the next twenty-seven years, I would rather have your willing cooperation than your forced resignation."

"Just sign it, Sean," Lizette said, her exhaustion present now even in her voice.

Sean looked at Lizette, as if betrayed. There was an unpredictability to Sean that suddenly felt much worse to Rubin. He was backed into a corner, and Rubin didn't know what he'd do.

"Sign it," Rubin said more gently. "You're not compromising anything by signing. It'll just make everything a lot easier."

Sean signed and passed the tablet to Lizette. She also signed but unlike Sean, her hand trembled as the stylus moved across the screen. Lizette held out the tablet to Rubin when she'd finished, the thin, electronic screen shaking with her hand.

"Thank you," Rubin said, receiving the device. He saved the document and slipped his tablet back into the desk drawer. Then Rubin pulled a pill bottle from his desk and walked over to Lizette. "When did you last eat?" he asked her.

She turned to Sean then back to Rubin and said, "I don't know."

Rubin took a pill from the bottle and held it out to her. Lizette took it between her thumb and forefinger and looked at it.

"It's the best meal replacement out there. You'll feel better after you take it," Rubin said.

Rubin offered one to Sean—he declined.

After Lizette swallowed the pill, she and Sean stood up, and Rubin led them down the hall to meet Sophia's doctors.

PART TWO

FIVE

Sophia rode her bicycle down the middle of a deserted, residential street. She was twenty-six and still didn't have her driver's license. Not that she wanted it. She liked her bike, especially in those moments when she was all alone with the wind and the sun, her long strawberry blond hair blowing backward. Sophia tilted her head up towards the sun and let the warmth caress her face.

It was hot out, but Sophia wore a long sleeve shirt to conceal her thanatometer. People were always checking out each other's PDAs, and then they'd either revere or sneer at what they saw. Nobody ever saw Sophia's thanatometer. She had a red piece of tape over its face to keep it that way. Only her doctors were allowed to see it, but—even though Dr. Ruiz had told her she needed a physical every year—Sophia hadn't been for a checkup in six years.

She let go of her handlebars and tried to balance on the solid line in the middle of the road. She slowly stretched her arms out wide, her pedaling more balanced and controlled now. Sophia squinted from the sun's glare before closing her eyes completely. Her heart began to beat faster. Suddenly dizzy, she teetered from side to side. But she didn't want to open her eyes. She breathed deeply through her nose, counting her breaths to centre her mind the way she used to when she had first learned to meditate. She didn't know where she was on the road, veering from the curb on the right to the row of parked cars on the left or miraculously still riding on the centre line.

Sophia continued to pedal and breathe. She feared crashing into something and wanted to open her eyes, but the deeper she breathed and the longer she kept her eyes shut, the less anything seemed to matter. Nothing existed, not pain or fear. She relaxed her face and let her head fall back further until she wasn't even on her bike anymore.

She sees herself floating through a never-ending meadow. As she moves through the golden grass, her beige cotton pants and black Beatles T-shirt turn into a sapphire blue dress with a large red bow at her waist. Then lightening flashes and, for a moment, the meadow becomes a field of cobblestones, but then the yellow grass quickly returns. Spooked, Sophia moves faster. The grass scrapes against her legs and feet like nettles, tearing her nylons, and burning her skin. Small scratches turn into bloody gashes as she flies faster and faster, farther and farther. The sky flashes again and again. She falls, the ground gives way beneath her, and she is consumed by darkness.

"Hey," a man shouted, running towards Sophia.

Sophia's eyes sprung open just in time to feel strong arms wrap around her waist from behind and lift her into the air. She grabbed hold of the arms squeezing her and pressed down hard, her long sleeves hiking up to reveal her thanatometer with the red tape on its display. Sophia's bike, now riderless, veered left, hit a parked car, and fell to the ground with its back tire spinning.

"What the hell's the matter with you," Sophia yelled, struggling to pry the arms off her waist. "Let go of me."

She kicked and railed until the man let go. When she hit the ground, she spun around to see who it was, her heart pounding. Sophia glared at the man. He glared back. His forehead and hair glistened with sweat. He wore a fluorescent blue spandex bodysuit with silver and gold bonded to its threads, making him almost sparkle in the sunlight. His sleek, black respirator and yellow-tinted sunglasses sat askew on his face, exposing his panting mouth and wild eyes.

"What are you doing riding down the middle of the street with your eyes closed?" he asked, his lips smushed to one side by his respirator. "And without both hands on your handlebars?" He glanced down at his thanatometer, pushed a button, and then wiped the sweat from his brow with the back of his hand.

Sophia pulled down the sleeve on her right arm to cover her own thanatometer and backed away from the man. She could feel the flush in her hot face and the dampness in her shirt sleeves where his sweaty arms had grabbed her.

"I'm just riding my bike," Sophia snapped, looking from his brown eyes to his blindingly white shoes.

"With your eyes closed down the middle of the street?" he asked. "I'd be surprised if stunts like that don't lower your PDA." The man looked down at his thanatometer again; Sophia grabbed hold of hers under her long sleeve and held it firm.

"God," he said, shaking his head and throwing his arms into the air. "Now my heart rate's accelerated above normal. And my routine's shot. I'll probably have to run for an extra half an hour to balance it out." He pointed at Sophia and said, "This better not bring my PDA down. I will not let you bring my PDA down."

"Oh what, a thousandth of a year? Relax," Sophia scoffed. "Your thana wouldn't even register it."

She pulled her sleeve away from her skin to dry his sweat. The feeling of the man's perspiration soaked into the fabric touching her skin made Sophia want to rip off her clothes and burn them.

"How could you disrespect your PDA like that kid?" he asked. "And mine?" The man began running on the spot. "Let me see your thanatometer," he said, reaching forward.

"No way," she said, swinging her arm behind her back.

"Listen," he began, "there's someone I think you should talk to. She specializes in renewed synchronicity between thanatometer and self. I'll give you her number; I think she could really help you."

"Go fuck yourself."

Sophia turned and moved towards her bike.

The man stopped running and said, "What did you say?" He fell in step behind her.

Sophia sensed his footsteps getting closer to her but she continued walking to her bike and bent down to pick it up. When she grabbed hold of the frame, the man seized her arm and pulled her up to face him.

"What did you say to me, kid?"

"I'm not a kid," Sophia growled, shaking off his hand and wiping her arm where he'd grabbed. "And don't ever touch me again."

His hands felt dirty even though they probably weren't. She wanted to shower and scrub him off of her forever. She'd even use her pumice stone if soap wasn't enough. She'd scrub and scrape until every trace of him was gone.

The man stood stunned for a second, looking at the revulsion in Sophia's face. When she turned to pick up her bike, he said, "Who are you? How do I know you?"

"You don't," Sophia said, looking her bike over and mounting it.

"No really, what's your name?"

Sophia sighed, stretched her sleeves down into her palms, and pressed down on her handlebars to keep them in place.

"None of your business," she said, riding towards the middle of the road.

"Hey kid," the man yelled after her. "You forgot to take the woman's number."

Sophia heard him running after her so she stood and pedaled harder.

The man stopped and shouted, "Ride on the path."

Sophia kept riding down the centre of the road and didn't look back.

SIX

Sophia stood in the foyer of Zack's building, waiting for him to answer his buzzer and staring at his name spelled out across the telecom screen.

"Come on. Be home," she said, tracing the letters of his name with her finger.

As the buzzer rang, Sophia looked back over her shoulder; she glanced down the street and wondered where she could go if Zack didn't answer. She turned back and began scrolling through the building directory. Any stranger would do but she focused on one name: "Sam," she whispered, before licking her lips.

She extended her finger to hang up on Zack and call Sam, but then Zack appeared on the screen.

"Oh hey," he said. "Come on up."

The door swung open automatically, and Sophia stepped inside. Going past the elevators, she threw open the stairwell door and ran up four flights—her breath quickening, her body just beginning to burn as she reached the top. She marched down the quiet, fourth floor hallway. The door to 407 was open. Without breaking stride, Sophia pushed on the door with both hands, slamming it against the hot sauce red walls of Zack's apartment hallway.

"Whoa! What was that?" Zack said, stepping around the corner and approaching Sophia. "Did you put a hole in the wall?"

When Zack was close enough to touch, Sophia pulled him close and kissed him. She pressed her tongue between his dry lips. Zack jerked his head back, but Sophia had his bottom lip between her teeth. He leaned farther back until his lip slipped through her bite. His mouth fell open.

"Jesus," he said. "Nice to see you too. Just let me, you know." He shut the door and checked for damage on the wall where the knob hit. He felt the wall for dents and said, "I'm surprised the doorknob didn't go right through the wall."

Sophia grabbed him again, shoved him against the wall, and mashed her lips against his. Zack didn't kiss her back until Sophia unbuckled his pants and took him in her hand. Then he opened his mouth and began exploring her feverish body with his hands.

Sophia felt the change in him and dropped to her knees, wanting him deep inside herself, wanting to devour him. Then she stood and hovered in front of Zack's face. When he leaned in to kiss her, she quickly turned around, her hair whipping his cheek. She dropped her pants and leaned back against him.

"Lie down," she said, while Zack kissed her neck.

When he hesitated, Sophia turned back to face him and pressed down on his shoulders; Zack lay down on the cool hard tile. Sophia straddled him and began gyrating and caressing her own body. Zack moaned and stared up at her.

She didn't want him to move, but he kept lifting his pelvis. Lay still, she wanted to say. But before she got a chance, Zack began throbbing inside her. He smiled, his body convulsing beneath her. He looked about ready to start sucking his thumb, so Sophia slapped him across the face. Zack smiled wider. Then she slapped him harder and his smile faded. She slapped him again and he grimaced. Again, and Zack tried to cover his face with his forearms. Sophia swung and swung, her hands turning Zack's arms as red as his face. Sophia's body burned hotter. She rocked back and forth, swinging and rocking, swinging and rocking. Her eyes squeezed shut and then, there was nothing. Just a blissful tingle all over her body. When her legs went numb, the rage melted away, and she felt Zack's hands grip her forearms.

"What's the matter with you?" Zack cried, sitting up, and wrapping his arms around Sophia. "Huh?" He held her close and rubbed her back.

Sophia opened her eyes and pushed away from him, making her butt hit the cold floor.

"Are you okay, Soph?" he asked, continuing to hold her arms.

His orgasm dripped out of her, and she felt like slapping him again. "Don't call me that," she said, twisting out of his grip. She stood up, turned her back to him, and started to dress.

"Why are you so pissed off all the time?" he asked. "Does hitting me make you feel better?"

Zack stood up, and Sophia turned to face him. Blood escaped his nose and ran towards his mouth. Watching the red moved down his face made her tingled between her legs.

Zack smeared the blood across the back of his hand, looked at it, and said, "God, Soph. Why'd you freak out on me?"

Sophia finished dressing and moved towards the door. Zack grabbed her arm from behind, but she shrugged him off.

"Don't touch me," she said without looking back.

"Come on, stay. Talk to me," he said. He held up his hands in front of him. "I won't touch you. Just tell me what's going on."

Sophia paused by the door and spun around. "You wanna know what's going on?"

"Of course I do," Zack said, calmly.

"This place is the problem."

"Why? What's wrong with it?"

"Assholes grabbing me off my bike for no reason and then yelling at me as if I'm the one who's done something wrong," Sophia said, stepping towards Zack.

"Who did that? Why'd they grab you?"

"Because I had my eyes closed. Okay. Big deal."

"Why were your eyes closed?"

"Why does it matter?" Sophia said. "He had no right to touch me."

Zack stepped towards her and said, "Is this about your thana?" He reached out for Sophia's wrist. "Can I see it?"

Sophia pulled her arm away. "No you can't see it," she said. "God, you're just like him. You're just like the rest of them." She turned and left, slamming the door behind her.

Zack opened the door and stuck his head out. "Wait," he said. "Come back. We'll meditate on it for a while."

Sophia ran down the stairwell and, when she reached outside, unlocked her bike. When she tried to mount her bike, she became dizzy and lost her balance. She stumbled back towards the brick wall of the building, her shoulder colliding with the hard clay blocks. After she had regained her strength, she shook her head and pushed away from the wall.

She tried to push her bike away from Zack's building but then her knees became wobbly and her arms trembled. Her eyes crossed slightly, unfocusing the world. She crouched down, lowered her head, and held the bike frame. Then she took a hand from the bike and pressed against her chest, her heartbeat was almost loud enough for her to hear it. Sophia closed her eyes, and the darkness spun violently.

She was eight and sprawled out on the manicured grass of her grandpa's front lawn beside her own throw up, her heart pounding, pounding, accelerating—unstoppable. Sophia closed her eyes and the world spun, so she opened them and the whirling stopped. She blinked slowly, her mum kneeled above her gently stroking her hair.

"It's okay, honey. You don't have to go back in if you don't want to," her mum said, pressing against Sophia's heaving chest with her other hand.

Her mum's soft palms made the nausea subside. Sophia closed her eyes and the darkness stilled. With eyes closed, Sophia wiped the vomit from her mouth with her sleeve.

Sophia opened her eyes and stared at her bike frame, breathing deeply, the metallic silver colour nauseating and too close. The queasy feeling she had was the same sensation she used to get at her grandfather's house, and she hadn't felt that way since the last time she saw the old man ten years ago. Sophia pictured him, his green eyes, the pulsating cables attached to computers that were extending his life. Every year there were more computers and cables and every year Sophia felt sicker to see her grandfather. Sophia imagined him lying in his bed, riddled with tubes attached to countless computers living for him. She retched and then jerked to the side and vomited onto the grass. When she finished, Sophia pressed her face into the cold metal of her bike frame, the chill soothing her. Sophia clung to the metal, pushed thoughts of her grandfather out of her mind, felt her heart slow down and the nausea subside. She opened her eyes, spit on the ground beside her tires, and staggered to her feet.

After slowly mounting her bike, Sophia rode away from the building down the middle of the street. The feeling of wet panties and the taste of puke made her ride home long and uncomfortable.

SEVEN

Drawing on a large tablet, Sophia sat cross-legged on the floor under her grandfather's dining table, staring down at the tip of her stylus as it moved across the screen. The tip of her tongue stuck out, as it usually did when she was concentrating, but not when her dad could see her.

"Suck your tongue back," he would say. "Dull-witted people do things like that, not smart girls like you."

Under the table, where nobody could see her, she was free to do what she wanted.

Sophia always began drawings by closing her eyes and scribbling for a few seconds. Then she would survey the scribbles before turning them into something recognizable. She never drew the same thing twice. Her latest drawing—which had started out as a sloppy, backwards ampersand—had become a killer whale swimming just below the surface of the ocean. As Sophia curved the smooth arch of the dorsal fin, she heard footsteps approach and stop right behind her. She slid her tongue back into her mouth, leaned forward to cover her drawing with both hands, and glanced over her shoulder to see her father's legs.

"What are you doing under there?" Sean asked.

"Nothing," Sophia said.

Sean sighed and bent down to look under the table. He saw a corner of Sophia's drawing and said, "Come out from under there and visit with your grandpa. We came here to see him, not to draw."

Sophia shook her head.

"Soph," Sean said, standing up straight. "You can draw at home. Come out. Now."

Sophia crawled out on the opposite side of the table from Sean with her tablet under one arm. She stood up and looked at him.

Sean pointed to the living room and said, "Leave that and go say hi."

Sophia reluctantly put the tablet on the table and, as she made her way to the living room, heard her dad pick up the tablet and walk toward the kitchen.

If he doesn't have to visit, why do I? Sophia thought. *I want my drawing back. It's not finished yet.*

Sophia entered the living room. Her grandfather sat in his chair while a nurse fiddled with his thanatometer, and her mum sat on the sofa across from him. Sophia moved to her mum's side and leaned up against her legs.

"Hey Sophie," Lizette said, placing her hand on Sophia's head. "Come to say hello?"

Sophia nodded, climbed onto the couch, and sat beside her mum.

"Why don't you come sit closer to me, Sophia," her grandfather said, gesturing to the empty chair next to him.

Sophia gazed at the chair without moving.

"Go on and sit next to your grandpa," Lizette said, gently pressing her palm against Sophia's back. "He barely gets to see you these days."

Sophia hopped down off the couch and, after dragging her feet six steps, lifted herself onto the chair beside her grandfather. He held his chin and regarded Sophia with his eyes squinted slightly, the nurse still beside him examining his thanatometer.

Sophia didn't notice him watching her. She was preoccupied with his thanatometer. Its display was much bigger than her own, with many more numbers that flashed constantly. Staring at it made her wrist itchy, so, with her index and middle fingers spread apart, she scratched the skin on both sides of her thanatometer to try and stop the tingle, but scratching only intensified the itch. When she scratched harder, she noticed the old man watching her and hid her arms behind her back and stared at her feet.

"Lizette," he said. "Why don't you let us have a moment alone."

"Good idea," Lizette said, standing up and turning to Sophia. "I'll be just in the other room, honey. Okay?"

"Go on. Go on," he said, waving Lizette away with the back of his hand. "We'll be fine." He watched Lizette leave the room and then turned to Sophia. "Does it itch?" he asked, leaning closer to her.

Sophia looked at his wide green eyes and then glanced over to where her mum had just exited the room.

"It itches doesn't it?"

She looked back at her grandpa again; he was squinting at her and his narrowed eyes made his crow's feet stretch out. Sophia nodded and then rested her eyes on the old man's thanatometer again.

He leaned back in his chair, clenched his teeth until his jaw muscles bulged, and sighed. "How old are you?" he asked.

"Eight," Sophia managed to say, even though her tongue clung to the roof of her mouth.

"Not in one hundred and twenty-seven years has mine ever made me itch," he said, gesturing to his thanatometer. "It's a part of my arm just as yours is. As soon as you accept that, your death age will start increasing."

The nurse stepped behind his chair and knelt down out of sight. Sophia could hear the clicking and beeping of a touch screen. The nurse reemerged holding a thick blue cable in one hand and connected it to the old man's thanatometer. When the cable began to glow and pulse, the nurse examined the thanatometer for a moment before leaving the room.

Sophia shifted in her seat. The glowing cable made her feel sick, but she still wanted to know what it was for. With her head tilted down, she followed the cable back behind the chair. Sophia leaned over slightly, trying to glimpse whatever was back there. She saw the corner of a heavy-looking black box with coloured lights flashing next to a digital display. Her heart began to beat faster, but Sophia leaned farther to see what was on the display.

"Don't look back there," her grandfather said.

Sophia quickly sat back in her chair. She looked from his green eyes to the cable to the box over and over until her stomach started to turn.

"Mind your manners, Sophia. If I wanted you to know what's behind me, I would have shown you. Okay?"

Without looking at him, Sophia nodded.

Sophia tried to focus on other things in the room, but her eyes kept returning to the pulsating cable, so she closed them and felt even more woozy.

"Now," he said, "if you want to politely ask me why I have my thanatometer hooked up to something, I would be happy to explain."

Sophia felt sick. To keep from throwing up, she squeezed her eyes shut tighter but then she retched and covered her mouth with both hands. Sophia sprung off the chair and ran from the room.

"Lizette," the old man hollered. "Your daughter's going to be sick."

"Sophia," Lizette called out, running around the corner just in time to see Sophia heading for the front door. "Are you okay?"

As soon as Sophia threw open the door and started down the outer steps, vomit pushed through her lips and fingers. Making it to the grass, she fell to her knees and emptied her stomach onto the manicured lawn. Then she flopped onto her back, everything still spinning.

Lizette rushed to Sophia, kneeled down beside her, and began stroking Sophia's hair.

"It's okay honey," Lizette said, resting her other hand on Sophia's chest. "You don't have to go back in if you don't want to."

"Mum, can we go home?" Sophia asked.

"We'll leave as soon as you feel ready to stand up," Lizette said.

Sophia felt ready but didn't want her mum's hands to leave her; they were soothing and made the dizziness subside. When the grass started to prickle her skin through her shirt, she sat up. Her mum helped her to her feet, held her close all the way to the car, and got into the back seat with her.

Sophia reclined and rested her head on her mother's lap. There she fell asleep before her father even sat down in the driver's seat.

EIGHT

At night and in the rain, Rubin sat inside his idling car with the heat on, waiting for Lizette in front of the Sip of Health a few blocks from her house. He thought she would be inside ordering a juice or seated by a window watching for him, but she wasn't. He was early though, but only because Lizette had told him to hurry, that she needed to see him right away, that it couldn't wait.

He had tried to get her to talk over the phone, but Lizette wouldn't. She wouldn't even meet at his office. If it had been anyone else on the other end of that phone, Rubin would have told them to call back on Monday to make an appointment. But not Sophia's mother when she sounded scared and as if holding back tears. Rubin never made house calls, but as soon as he hung up the phone he left his office to meet Lizette. From the urgency in her voice, he figured she would have been waiting for him.

It was an unusually cold and wet autumn. Rubin looked down the street leading to the Nolan house. Beneath the lamppost light, rain pelted the deserted street and sidewalks. Rubin watched the rain and hoped Sophia was okay. If it were something life threatening, he was sure Lizette would've called an ambulance.

Sudden knocking on his passenger side window made Rubin jump. He turned to see Lizette peering at him through the window. He pushed a button, the door swung up slowly, the dome light illuminated the interior of the car, and Lizette hurried inside. She was soaked. Water dripped from the clumped ends of her matted hair, the tip of her nose, and the sleeves of her sopping sweater, made big by the rainwater.

"Why are you all wet?" Rubin asked. "Where's your car? How'd you get here?"

Lizette was panting. She swallowed hard and said, "I ran."

"Why? What's going on? Is Sophia okay?"

"She's fine," Lizette said, huffing. "This isn't about her." She sniffed and then continued, "Well, I guess it kind of is." She wiped her nose on her soggy sleeve, sniffed again, and said, "Everything's about her now isn't it?"

The door closed behind Lizette automatically, shutting out the rain but not the wet. Almost the entire passenger side of Rubin's car was soaked. He knew moisture was collecting on the seat beneath Lizette; he was willing to help her but not if it meant ruining his upholstery. Rubin didn't speak. He listened to the rain pounding against the exterior of the car and watched Lizette drip all over the interior.

Lizette shivered. "Sorry to make you meet me like this," she said, her teeth chattering slightly. "I just don't have anyone to …"

Rubin felt suddenly angry with himself for having petty thoughts. He was in the healthcare field for God's sake, and his first concern was for his seat covers? He turned up the heat and reached into the backseat for his gym bag. The rear windows were completely fogged up, the haze creeping forward onto the other windows. When he sat back down in his seat, Rubin held his towel and gym clothes in his hands.

"Here, dry off," he said, passing her the towel. "It's clean. I didn't workout today."

"Thanks," Lizette said, taking the towel and sinking her face into it.

"These socks are clean too," he said, holding up his gym clothes. "But I've worn the shirt and shorts once." He sniffed the shirt; it stank, but he had nothing else to offer her. "At least they're dry," he said.

Lizette finished drying her hair and face before trying to slip off her heavy sweater. It clung to her body, and Rubin watched her struggle for a moment before reaching out and holding onto one of her sleeves so she could slip her arm out. Once both of her arms were free, Rubin helped her lift the sloppy sweater up, covering her face and exposing her navel, black bra, and throat. Under the dome light's glow, Rubin could see that goosebumps covered her moist skin. His gaze lingered on Lizette's naked skin while she raised the sweater over her head and face. When she emerged and tossed her mushy sweater onto the mat beneath her feet, Rubin looked away. The windows were completely fogged now, so Rubin turned up the heat again.

"Thanks," she said, drying off and slipping on his gym shirt.

"No problem," Rubin said, staring at the windshield. "Warmer?"

"Much."

"Why'd you run here in this?" Rubin turned to her and asked. "We could have met at my office tomorrow. Where it's dry."

Lizette put her hair up. "I need your help," she said, before letting her hands flop down onto her lap.

"Okay," Rubin said, nodding. "With what? I mean if Sophia's fine than I'm not sure what—"

"I'm pregnant."

Rubin held his breath for a second before saying, "How? Are you sure?"

Lizette reached into her wet pocket and pulled out a tiny, metallic disc with the symbol of mars on both sides. She held it out to Rubin and said, "Positive."

Rubin took the pregnancy disc and examined it. Confused, he said, "Did you start taking your fertility medication again?"

"No, not after Sophia."

"Then how were you able to conceive?"

"I don't know. It just happened."

Rubin stared down at the symbol of mars and rubbed his temples.

"It's a boy," Lizette said, nodding to the disc with a weary smile.

Rubin looked up at Lizette; he didn't smile back. "Where did you get this thing?" he asked. "I haven't seen one for years."

"A friend. Why?"

"Can it be traced back to you?"

"I don't know. Why?"

"Where did your friend get it from?" he asked, raising his voice, annoyed that all outdated pregnancy tests hadn't been returned to National Wellness for incineration.

Lizette drew back from Rubin, her shoulders pressing up against the passenger side door. "It was just an old one that she had okay," Lizette said, starting to feel claustrophobic and regret coming to Rubin. "One she hadn't used."

"Can you trust her?" Rubin said, his voice calm and soft again.

"Of course."

"Then tell her to forget she gave it to you. If anyone asks, anyone who knew about it, she lost it. Okay?"

"Okay."

Rubin looked down at the disc and said, "I'll head back to my office tonight to incinerate it."

"Why? I'm not going to have him," Lizette said.

"You're not?" Rubin said, sinking back into his seat, shocked and relieved that he wouldn't have to convince her to terminate.

"No. I mean, how could I, after Sophia?" Lizette said, wiping drips of water from her forehead. "She threw up again, you know."

"When?"

Lizette sniffed and rubbed her eyes. "A few days ago at her grandpa's house."

"She's an anxious kid," Rubin said. "Her doctors say it's just nerves."

Lizette crossed her arms, shivered, and said. "It feels like more than nerves when she's convulsing in my arms." She swallowed hard. "I look through her vomit for blood and when I don't find any, I think it'll come the next time. Or I think that the next time it'll be all blood, and I'll look through the red for half-digested food." She brushed a few straggling hairs off her face.

"Sophia still has a lot of time left," Rubin said. "And maybe even more after that. You'll torture yourself if you worry about it all the time."

"Don't you think about it?"

Rubin hesitated before nodding.

"Are you torturing yourself or are you just normal to worry about it?"

Lizette undid her pants and kicked them off onto the sweater at her feet. Rubin stared at the fogged up windshield as she dried herself with the towel and then put on his shorts.

She sighed and said, "Sophia is starting to ask questions about it. About all the doctors appointments and the numbers and what they mean."

"What do you tell her?"

"I don't know. Nothing. I avoid the questions. Sean wants to cover up her thanatometer to try and achieve some sort of placebo effect," Lizette said, shaking her head. "He still thinks he can add a hundred years to it … to her."

"Do you think it'll work?"

"I hope," she said, wringing her hands. "But I know she'll die before me. And I don't want to have to watch a second child die too."

Rubin placed his hand in hers.

Lizette squeezed his hand, her eyes watery. "That's why I called you," she said. "I need you to stop it."

Rubin squeezed back. "Does Sean know?" he asked.

Lizette shook her head and mopped her eyes. "No, and he never will," she said.

Rubin nodded and glanced down at Lizette's soaked clothes lying on the car mat before turning back to the windshield. He lifted his hand from Lizette's and wiped away the haze just above the steering wheel—it was still pouring outside. While Rubin watched the rain pummel his car, he thought of Sean. He knew keeping Lizette's pregnancy from him was the best thing to do. Telling him would only complicate things. Sean would probably try to stop the abortion if he knew, especially for a son; he seemed like the patriarchal type.

Rubin turned back to Lizette. She hadn't been sleeping, her eyes were glazed and appeared sunken.

She reminded Rubin of how Claudia, his ex-wife, looked the day they decided to get a divorce.

Had Claudia kept a pregnancy from me? Had she gone to our doctor to abort it? Was the procedure done at my hospital while I was working?

Claudia could have done it without telling him, and it would have been the right thing to do for her and the baby because he only would have complicated things. But he still had a right to know. Even if he couldn't have stopped an abortion, he deserved to know. And so did Sean, but Rubin wasn't going to tell him, even though he wanted to.

"How far along are you?" Rubin asked.

"Three weeks tomorrow," she said, biting her lower lip. "Can you, you know, stop it?"

"I could have stopped it two years ago," he said, shaking his head. "Or at least taken away your fertility pills."

"I told you, I didn't take any," Lizette snapped. "And what do you mean you could have stopped it two years ago?"

Rubin sighed and looked into Lizette's eyes. "Your procreation permission was suspended after Sophia's birth," he said. "I couldn't tell you at the time. Not after everything you went through."

"Suspended? For how long?"

"Indefinitely."

"What?" she said, breathing heavily through her mouth again, her voice shaking with anger.

"They didn't want another Sophia to be born."

"But they can't do that," Lizette said, shifting in her seat and wiping away tears. "It's, it's not our fault Sophia's PDA is so low. And they don't even know the cause. How can they just revoke our right to have children?"

"They don't care about any of that. You have no rights as far as they're concerned," Rubin said. "It's a precautionary measure for them. They can't explain Sophia's PDA, so they don't want you to get pregnant again. For them it's simple."

Lizette sniffed and sat up straight. "I'll fight it," she said.

"How?"

"It violates our rights. We were approved to have children over eight years ago and nothing has changed. We're just as healthy."

"Sophia changed everything."

"It's not right," Lizette said, her anger giving way to despair. She placed her hands on her belly and looked down. "I don't know. Maybe I should keep it. Maybe I don't have to …"

"Wait a second," Rubin said, his tone cautious but assertive. "You just said you didn't want another child right?"

"Yeah but that's when it was still my decision," she said, rubbing her belly. "This baby might be normal. Maybe I shouldn't abort."

"Lizette, I don't know what they'll do if they find out you're pregnant. They might not want to abort the pregnancy. They might want to turn you and your baby into lab rats, quarantine you for nine months and perform every test imaginable. Is that what you want?"

Lizette shook her head.

"Then we need to abort the pregnancy as soon as possible. It's still your decision. Forget about National Wellness."

Lizette buried her face in her hands. "I know. You're right," she said, emerging from her palms. "But having my permit suspended changes everything."

Rubin closed his eyes and gripped the steering wheel. "I'm sorry I didn't tell you sooner," he said. "I thought I could tell you if and when you decided to have another child. I don't know. When you came in for more fertility medication or something. I didn't expect you to get pregnant without it. The medication must still be in your system somehow."

"I still have some pills. But I swear I didn't take any."

"May I have them," Rubin asked, facing her.

Lizette shook her head.

"Will you incinerate them then?"

"No."

"Fine," Rubin said, gripping the steering wheel tighter. "If you go through with the termination, I'll let you keep the fertility drugs. But, if you ever decide that you want another child, you have to talk to me before you use them. Okay? I don't know if I'll be able to get your PPP reinstated but I will do everything I can when you're ready."

Still holding her belly, Lizette turned to look out the window.

Rubin stared at her and said, "Lizette?"

"Fine," she said without looking at him, her voice flat. "But I wanna keep the disc."

"I'm sorry, I can't let you do that. I have to get rid of it."

Lizette turned to Rubin, tears streaking down her stricken face. "I need to keep the disc," she said, sniffing and using the heel of her hand to wipe away tears. "I need something of … his."

"I'm sorry but you can't have it," Rubin said, slipping the disc into his pocket. "The risk of Sean finding it isn't worth it."

Lizette cried into the towel and then wiped her face and nose with it. "Fine. Fine," she said. "But don't incinerate it."

"I have to."

"Hide it in your office somewhere. Please. For me. I need to know it still exists. Please Rubin," said, holding his hand again.

"Okay," he said. "I'll keep it for you."

She reclined in her seat and said, "Thank you."

Lizette closed her eyes. Rubin sighed.

"When do you want to take care of this," Rubin asked softly.

"Can we do it tonight?" Lizette said, her voice regaining its normal charm. "Sean'll be at the pool with Sophia for the next two hours."

"He's teaching her to swim?" Rubin asked.

Lizette chuckled and said, "It's part of her training. I swear that girl is going to be a world-class triathlete when Sean's done with her."

Rubin smiled and noticed that the steam on the windows had melted away.

"We'll have to go to my office," he said.

"Let's go. I'm ready."

Rubin held down a button on the steering wheel and said, "Office." When he released the button, Lizette's seatbelt buckled and the car began moving forward.

As they drove away from the juice place, Lizette said, "How long will it take?"

"You'll miscarry right away," Rubin said, glancing in his rearview mirror. "Have you ever taken the pill before?"

"Never."

"Well, because you're only in the first month, it'll just be like the first day of your period. You may experience some spotting and more severe crapping though, but that's nothing to worry about."

Lizette stared out the windshield.

"We can dry your clothes when we get to my office," Rubin said, glancing at his smelly clothes that Lizette was wearing. "That way you won't have to go home in those."

She smiled and thanked him. "Do you have kids?" Lizette asked.

93

Rubin shook his head; he didn't takes his eyes off the road.

"Married?"

"Divorced."

"Oh. I'm sorry."

"Don't be," Rubin said, turning the heat down again. He had started to sweat. "We'll be there in about twenty minutes."

It continued to pour as they made their way towards Rubin's office. Neither of them spoke the rest of the way. While Rubin watched the windshield wipers move back and forth to clear away the rain, he thought about how best to get the pill out of the pharmacy, give it to Lizette, and get her back home without anyone noticing. After he'd planned it out, he turned to Lizette to tell her how they would proceed, but she had fallen asleep. She looked peaceful, so Rubin didn't wake her. He turned the heat off and drove on in silence.

NINE

On the thirtieth floor of the National Wellness Executive Offices Building and inside the largest corner office in the building, Rubin and Claudia sat on a couch facing Tabitha's desk, waiting for the CEO to return from her meeting. The two far walls of the office were all glass, providing an unobstructed view of the northern half of the city. Even though sunlight poured in through the windows, the office was cold: air conditioning overpowered the sun's warmth.

Claudia surveyed the room, feeling as if she were in an executive hotel suite. She wondered if a bedroom or a bathroom was behind the closed door to her right. Different types of chairs and tables, more art than functional furniture, filled the office. There were fig trees in every corner and a single sculpture, beside Tabitha's desk, of a naked female torso with numerous diagonal stripes cut out of it.

Rubin watched Claudia. She bit the inside of her bottom lip while staring at the sculpture, a nervous habit she'd had when Rubin met her five years ago. He placed his hand on her thigh and squeezed. When she looked at him, Rubin smiled. Claudia smiled back—a forced smile that quickly faded—and placed her hand on his, her sweaty palm moistening Rubin's knuckles.

"There's nothing to worry about," Rubin said. "This is all routine."

Claudia took her hand from Rubin's.

"What?" Rubin asked.

"Why are we here? Huh? Everyone picks up their triple P from the registry. Not from the," Claudia lowered her voice and said, "the CEO of National Wellness."

"Honey, relax," Rubin said, wrapping his arm around her and pulling her closer to him. "She's my boss. She probably just wants to be the first to congratulate us. It's all part of working here. They make a big deal out of their employees getting permits. Just think of it as a privilege."

Claudia crossed her legs and sighed. "I'm sure you're right," she said, leaning against Rubin and resting her head on his shoulder.

Rubin kissed the top of Claudia's head just as he heard Tabitha's voice outside the office.

"She's here," he said, turning around to see Tabitha standing just outside the office talking with her assistant.

Claudia sat up straight and adjusted her skirt. Rubin stood up and stepped towards the open door. As Tabitha entered the office, carrying a tablet under her arm, she approached Rubin with her hand held out.

"Rubin," she said, smiling apologetically. "Sorry to keep you waiting."

Rubin shook her hand and said, "Oh we weren't waiting long." He then gestured to Claudia. "You remember my wife, Claudia."

Claudia stood up and moved towards Tabitha with her hand extended.

As the women shook hands, Tabitha said, "Of course I do. I haven't seen you for awhile. You look very well. How's your PDA? Any new increases since we last spoke?"

Claudia glanced at Rubin before responding. "It goes up by a day every twenty-fours days or so. A month every two years," she said, glancing down at her thanatometer.

"That's good. Above average," Tabitha said, nodding her approval. "At that rate, you might outlive your husband here."

Tabitha laughed and placed her hand on Rubin's forearm. Claudia smiled and rubbed his back.

Rubin chuckled and said, "We're actually trying for the same PDA. Right, honey?" He looked to Claudia, who nodded and allowed her smile to fade. "And we're on pace too," Rubin added.

"Interesting," Tabitha said, still smiling. "I didn't think you were a romantic, Rubin."

Rubin shrugged and said, "It just makes sense."

"So, you don't mind never reaching your optimal PDA?" Tabitha asked, becoming more serious.

Rubin took Claudia's hand in his, looked at her, and said, "The most important thing is being together."

"Right," Claudia said before nibbling the inside of her bottom lip.

"Well, shall we get to why you're here," Tabitha said, motioning to the couch in front of her desk. "Please have a seat."

Still holding hands, Rubin and Claudia sat back down.

Tabitha shut her office door, sat behind her desk, and placed her tablet in front of her. "So," she began, "I'm sorry about asking you to come here to receive the results of your procreation permit assessment. But with Rubin in line to become the next COO at National Wellness, we've been extremely thorough with your application."

Tabitha looked down at her tablet and began scrolling. "First of all," she said, looking at Rubin. "I'd just like to thank you, Rubin, for your exceptional work these past six years. Your record was impeccable before you began at National Wellness and you've maintained that level of excellence since coming here."

"Thank you. I appreciate that," Rubin said, grinning.

Claudia beamed and snuggled up closer to Rubin.

"Now," Tabitha said, scanning her tablet and scrolling again, "about your assessment."

Tabitha turned her attention to the Russells, interlaced her fingers, and rested her hands on her tablet screen. "As you already know, you are both extremely healthy individuals with robust genealogies," she said, making periodic eye contact with each of them. "However, your DNA tests revealed that you are both unaffected carriers of an autosomal recessive disorder."

Rubin let go of Claudia's hand. He leaned forward with his forearms pressed into his thighs. "Which one?" he asked.

"Thalassemia."

Rubin buried his face in his hands.

"What does that mean?" Claudia asked, alternating her panicked gaze between Rubin and Tabitha.

Rubin sat up straight and turned to Claudia. "We both have the recessive gene for a blood disorder," he said.

Claudia shook her head and scoffed at the idea. "What kind of blood disorder?"

"One where hemoglobin isn't synthesized normally," Rubin said.

Claudia turned to Tabitha. "I don't understand. We don't have the disorder, right?" she asked.

"That's right," Tabitha said. "You're both completely healthy. But because you both have this recessive gene, your children would have a fifty percent chance of also having it and a twenty-five percent chance of actually developing the disease. Do you understand?"

"Yeah," Claudia replied, "but what does that mean for our permit?"

"It means," Rubin began, taking both of Claudia's hands in his, "that we've been denied."

"But isn't there?" Claudia said, beginning to cry. "Can't we …?"

Rubin hugged her and said, "It's okay honey. We have other options."

Claudia sobbed uncontrollably in Rubin's arms, her face pressed against his shoulder. Rubin held her tight. He couldn't stop her from trembling nor could he stop her tears from soaking into his shirt. He wished Tabitha would leave; he could sense her eyes on him and Claudia, seeing what they shouldn't. As Claudia continued to sob and his boss continued to sit there, Rubin turned and looked at Tabitha; her expression was one of pity, and it made Rubin want to spit in her face.

Tabitha pulled a handkerchief from a drawer and walked around her desk with it. "Here take this," she said, holding out the handkerchief to Claudia.

Rubin took it and handed the handkerchief to his wife, who buried her face into it.

"I'm very sorry," Tabitha said. "If only one of you were a carrier of the gene, then your children would be safe from developing the disease. They would still have a fifty-fifty chance of having the gene passed on to them, but you still would have qualified for a permit."

"So that's it," Claudia said, mopping her face with the handkerchief. "We can't have children?"

Tabitha crossed her arms. "I didn't say that," she said. "Currently, you and Rubin are not compatible for procreation, but there is always gene therapy."

"Right," Rubin said. "We can get gene therapy to eliminate the disorder."

"Exactly. One or, preferably, both of you can undergo gene therapy and then you can reapply for a procreation permit," Tabitha said.

"How long will all that take?" Claudia asked.

"Six months to a year," Tabitha said.

Claudia's face drooped down even further. She suddenly appeared haggard to Rubin, and he knew it was the thought of waiting another year that dispirited her.

"One year isn't so bad," he said.

Claudia didn't respond. She simply stood up and left the office, wiping her eyes with the handkerchief.

Rubin glanced at Tabitha before, without thanking her or saying goodbye, standing up and hurrying after his wife.

"Rubin," Tabitha said as she watched him leave the room.

But Rubin didn't turn back. He didn't care if his boss thought less of him because he ignored her or because of how his wife reacted or because he had a bad recessive gene. In that moment, he only cared about Claudia, and she needed him.

TEN

Inside a bleach white examination room with one of her doctors standing beside her, Sophia lay down on a stainless steel examining table. She gasped for breath as the cold metal pressed against her back and was thankful for the thin barrier her T-shirt made between her bare skin and the freezing metal. Her muscles flexed and twitched involuntarily as she reclined fully. Sophia crossed her arms firmly across her chest and exhaled as if submerging herself in an icy bath. After the table had begun to absorb some of her body heat, she began to relax.

"Give me your wrist, Sophia," Dr. Salina Ruiz said, holding out her hand.

Sophia looked at the doctor's open palm and then allowed her eyes to move up the long sleeve of her lab coat to her face and tightly pulled-back dark hair. She was a slight, wiry woman with the skin of a sixty-something exerciseoholic who ran five marathons every year—her facial bones protruded beneath her taut skin making her eyes bulge. Skeleton Face, Sophia called her. She had given Dr. Ruiz the nickname after their first checkup together when Sophia was three years old and terrified of the unnaturally thin lady with veiny hands and bony fingers.

Now sixteen, Sophia wasn't afraid of Skeleton Face anymore, just disgusted; she didn't like looking at her but at the same time she couldn't look away. Whenever she stared at Skeleton Face for too long, Sophia got the urge to poke her skin to find out if it felt like plastic.

"Come on," Dr. Ruiz said. "Don't worry, I won't take the tape off your thanatometer."

Sophia wasn't worried about the black tape covering the display; after hooking up to her thanatometer, Skeleton Face would be able to see through it anyway. Sophia held out her arm to the doctor and stared at the ceiling. She missed the warmth of her mother's hand holding her own. She even missed her father standing in the corner of the room with his arms crossed over his chest. Her parents were in the waiting room for the first time in sixteen years. At Sophia's last checkup one year before, Dr. Ruiz had said that Sophia was old enough to start receiving unaccompanied examinations. "She is a young woman after all."

At the time, Sophia had agreed. Solo exams meant freedom and independence and adulthood. But as Dr. Ruiz strapped her arm down onto the examination table, Sophia regretted her decision. She glanced from the ceiling to the door and wished her parents would burst in and take their customary positions—her mum beside the bed and her dad with his back against the closed door. But the door remained shut, and, all alone, Sophia watched Skeleton Face extend a cable from the side of the table. She closed her eyes, took a deep breath, and heard the cable connect to her thanatometer. Electricity surged through Sophia's body, making her jerk. She felt electrocuted every time the cable was hooked up to her.

Sophia opened her eyes and looked at her thanatometer; at the edges of the tape, its display grew bright and then dimmed over and over again as if it had its own heartbeat. Dr. Ruiz sat down on a stool beside the table. She observed the cable connection for a few seconds before pulling a computer screen on an extendable arm up from the side of the examination table and positioning it in front of her. She stared at the screen, scrolling and typing.

"I need to take a blood sample, Sophia," she said from behind the screen. "It'll just be a little prick."

Dr. Ruiz pulled a steel pen-shaped syringe, with no visible needle, from the side of the computer screen, pushed the computer aside, and leaned closer to Sophia. "Extend your index finger towards me please."

Sophia did as told. The steel pressed into her finger right before she felt a sudden prick. It didn't hurt, her entire body felt a bit numb from the cable's electricity, but she still bled.

"Squeeze this with your index finger and thumb," Dr. Ruiz said, placing a swab on the tiny puncture hole.

While Sophia squashed the swab between her fingers, Dr. Ruiz faced the screen again, inserted the syringe into it, and began typing on the screen. The incessant tapping of her fingernails on glass filled the quiet examining room. To Sophia, it felt as if the doctor were tapping on her forehead, the kind of torture she heard siblings inflicted on each other while trying to extract the names of ten cities; Sophia couldn't think of anything except breaking the doctor's fingers.

"Can I go?" Sophia asked, lifting up her head and wanting to rip the straps from her restrained arm.

"Well, that depends," Dr. Ruiz said, pushing the screen aside again and leaning forward. "Do you have anything you'd like to tell me?"

"No."

"Have you had any more bouts of nausea? Any more vomiting?"

"No."

"That's not what your mother tells me."

Sophia wanted to scream. She hated questions about how she felt. Her parents usually answered for her; they had more to say about how she felt then she did. Sophia wished they would appear in the room to talk to Skeleton Face. She wished she could go back to being just a thanatometer.

Sophia rested her head on the table again with a thud and then struck the back of her head against the metal a few more times before responding. "Can you unhook me please?"

"Of course. We're all finished," Dr. Ruiz said, disconnecting the cable from Sophia's thanatometer.

As soon as the current running through her stopped, Sophia felt normal again. She quickly sat up and, lightheaded, went blind for a moment, so she sat completely still until her vision returned.

"Everything checks out fine," Dr. Ruiz said.

Sophia turned towards the doctor's voice and vision returned. Skeleton Face had her hands on her hips and shook her head with a confused look on her face.

"You are a healthy sixteen-year-old girl," she said. "Does that make you happy to hear that?"

"I guess so. Can I go now please?" Sophia asked again.

"Yes, yes you can go. Unless," she said, stepping in front of Sophia, "you want to talk about the nausea."

"It's no big deal," Sophia said, looking at Dr. Ruiz. "I just, get myself worked up sometimes. Like you said before."

Dr. Ruiz stared back at Sophia, nodding without speaking. Sophia glanced at the door and began swinging her legs and banging her heels against the table.

"Well, whenever you feel anxious," Dr. Ruiz said, speaking over the racket. She then stepped forward and put her hands on Sophia's knees. "Could you stop that please?"

Sophia stopped. Skeleton Face was inches from her face now. Too close to look at, so she turned to the wall.

"Thank you," Dr. Ruiz said, removing her hands from Sophia's knees. "Please, Sophia. Look at me."

Sophia turned back and stared into the bony face and bug eyes.

"Now, whenever you feel anxious, just focus on your breathing and know that the nausea you feel is under your control. Can you do that for me, Sophia?"

"What?" Sophia asked, pretending she wasn't listening.

Dr. Ruiz exhaled loudly through her nose, blinked slowly, and said, "Know that you're in control of your nausea and can stop it when it happens?"

Sophia nodded—that initial fear of Skeleton Face she had had when she was three years old resurfaced and made her mouth dry up. She looked for the door, but the doctor was obscuring it.

"Well then," Dr. Ruiz said, standing up straight and stepping aside. "You're free to go."

Sophia jumped down off the table and hurried to the outer room where her parents sat waiting for her. She was happy to see them and almost hugged her mother before thinking better of it.

On the car ride home, sitting in the back seat, Sophia stared out the window and told her parents that she preferred solo checkups. That she should've had them all along. She wanted them to say that she shouldn't get used to it because they were going in with her next time, like before. She wanted to fight with them in vain until she finally had to accept their decision. But her father said he was glad that the checkup went well, and her mother didn't say anything at all.

Sophia didn't speak the rest of the way home, her throat burned from holding back tears, and she was ashamed that she felt like crying. Children cried, and she wasn't a child anymore.

ELEVEN

In his office, after everyone else had gone home for the day hours before, Rubin paced, dictating to the tablet propped up on a stand in the middle of his desk. As he spoke, the cursor transcribed.

"There continue to be absolutely no irregularities in Sophia Nolan's physiology. As the most recent comprehensive physical examination attests, she continues to maintain an optimal level of health while her predicted death age remains unnaturally low. It can be assumed, based on the in-depth evaluations made by her various physicians over the past sixteen years, that Sophia Nolan will maintain this optimal level of health until her twenty-seventh birthday when it is hypothesized, based on her thanatometer readout, that she will undergo accelerated organismal senescence and die of a specific proximal cause such as acute liver failure. As of yet, however, her cells have not become senescent."

Rubin sat down and read over what he had just dictated. All of his reports paraphrased the initial report he had written when Sophia was born. There was nothing new to add, and he was running out of new ways of saying the same thing. Nothing new had been discovered that would definitively answer the two most important questions about Sophia: why was her PDA so low? And what would happen to her at twenty-seven? Rubin selected his latest report with his index finger and dragged it to the trash can in the corner of the screen, holding it there for a moment; he thought about putting a current date on the previous report and resubmitting it, but everyone would notice. Rubin dragged the document away from the trash, took his hand from the screen, and put his hands behind his head. Leaning back and gazing up at the lights above him, he spun around in his chair.

"Blah, blah, blah, blah, blah. Who the hell knows what'll happen to her? Maybe she'll spontaneously combust," Rubin said. "Nobody has any idea. She probably won't even die at twenty-seven, but nobody can say that because that would mean something even worse than a person dying of old age one hundred years premature."

Rubin stopped spinning. He faced his tablet screen and skimmed over what he'd just said—he preferred it for its honesty, so he continued.

"What if ... she's the first to have evolved beyond thanatometers?" he said, watching his words—slightly delayed—appear behind the cursor.

What would that mean? he thought, rubbing his chin and reading his question over and over.

Rubin highlighted his diatribe, deleted it, and closed his report. Open on his screen behind the report was Dr. Ruiz's assessment and behind that Sophia's current thanatometer readout. Nothing had changed. She had the vital signs of someone who'd live to be one hundred and thirty. Rubin tapped on the locator tab at the bottom of the thanatometer readout; a tiny map popped up with a flashing blue dot in the centre—it was Sophia and she wasn't at home. Rubin zoomed down to street level and was then looking at a brick, apartment building, the blue dot flashing in the basement.

Probably at a friend's house.

He closed the map and the remote access to Sophia's thanatometer. A picture of Sophia was still open on the screen. Rubin touched the photo and zoomed in. Sophia stared at him.

He had taken the picture from his car, at about seventy-five yards away, during one of Sophia's soccer games. She wore a yellow uniform and had just passed the ball cross field to avoid two defenders in red rushing her at the edge of the picture. Her eyes must have been following the ball, but she appeared to be looking directly at the camera. After Rubin had snapped the picture, he had felt as if Sophia had seen him with the camera lens propped against the half-open car window. At the time, he had quickly driven away, convinced that in fact Sophia hadn't seen him.

Rubin cropped the picture around Sophia and zoomed in. Then he selected just her face and zoomed in until her eyes filled the tablet screen. There, in his office, she stared at him, and Rubin became convinced that she had actually seen him. Across the field, beyond the game, through the bleachers, on the far side of the street, she had seen him.

Rubin closed the picture and opened a folder with fifteen other pictures in it. He had captured Sophia at every age. As he scrolled through the pictures, Sophia getting older and older as he did, Rubin realized that she had eyed the camera in almost every image. He had tried to capture her looking in his direction, but she appeared to be staring right at him, as if to say, I know what you're doing.

Rubin grabbed his tablet, put it flat on his desk— screen side down—and stood up. He needed to leave his office. As he did so, he felt like a fraud. He had no right to spy on Sophia and take covert pictures of her. Tabitha would reprimand him if she knew, maybe even reassign him. But the posed pictures provided by her parents weren't good enough. They were contrived, and Rubin needed to see Sophia as she really was. And now, she had seen him.

Moving towards his car in the underground parkade, he imagined her eyes watching him. He glanced around expecting to see the glint of a camera lens behind one of the concrete pillars or in one of the dark corners, but there wasn't anyone spying on him.

When Rubin sat down in the driver's seat and the door closed behind him, he snickered at his own ridiculous paranoia. He knew Sophia wasn't spying on him but he couldn't escape the feeling that she knew he was spying on her. He would be more careful in the future. Nobody, especially Sophia, could know how close he had gotten to her.

It was almost midnight by the time he pulled into his driveway. Just when he shut off his car, his phone rang; it was an incoming call from the Nolan house. He contemplated not answering but knew he had to.

"Hello."

"Rubin, it's Lizette. I'm so glad you answered."

"Is everything okay?"

"No, it's Sophia. She's not home yet and nobody's seen her since this afternoon."

"Is she at a friend's?"

"We don't know where she is," Lizette said before pausing. "Can you come here?"

Rubin didn't respond right away. He wanted to go to bed. He had hoped not to think about Sophia for the rest of the night.

"I know it's late but," Lizette said, "but we just don't know what to do. Or who else to call."

"I'll be right there," Rubin said.

"Thank you."

Rubin hung up, started his car, and said, "The Nolan house," into his navigation system. As his car reversed, he reached for his tablet to check Sophia's locator; he wanted to see if she was on her way home; running into her was the last thing he needed. His tablet was usually in its case on the passenger seat, but it wasn't there. He had left it at his office. Rubin suddenly felt like an idiot. He thought about stopping to grab it before going to the Nolans', but it was in the opposite direction, so he decided to quickly stop in to assure them that Sophia was okay and then go back to his office to find out exactly where she was. Rubin just prayed that Sophia wouldn't catch him at her house.

TWELVE

Soaked with sweat, hands clenched into tight fists, Sophia—barely able to hear the distant cheers of the crowd over her quick, heavy breaths and the sound of clay crunching beneath the soles of her sneakers—raced towards the finish line. She was sixteen and competing in the last meet of the season.

As she rounded the final corner, only two runners were ahead of her; number nineteen in second place and number twenty-two in first. Sophia ran harder, moving into second place just behind the leader. When the finish line was directly in front of her, Sophia sprinted faster, stuck out her chest, and won the race. She threw her arms in the air and stopped running. Pacing with her hands on her hips, she tried to catch her breath.

Sean stood in front of the bleachers at the edge of the track. "Good hard run, Soph," he yelled, clapping.

Sophia walked over to her father and grabbed the water bottle and towel from the bench beside him.

"Great run," Sean said. "Great run."

Sophia sat down on the bench and began to breathe more slowly. "Nadia … is fast," she said before squirting water into her mouth and wiping her face with the towel.

Sean sat down beside her. "Yeah," he said, "but you're faster." He smiled and patted her leg. "I think we're ready, don't you?"

"For what?" she asked, hiding her thanatometer, black tape covering its display, from her father.

"You know what," he said, reaching out to her and grinning. "You won. So before you go get your trophy let's pull that tape off and give you a real prize."

Sophia glanced at all the people hustling around the track, most of them competitors with numbers on their shirts. She ignored her dad when she noticed Nadia, number twenty-two, approaching her.

"Nice run," she said, extending her hand to Sophia.

Sophia stood up and shook the girl's hand. "Thanks. You too."

When Nadia walked away, Sophia sat back down.

Sean watched the girl leave, snickered, and said, "Loser," under his breath before turning back to Sophia smirking.

Sophia buried her face in the towel and groaned.

"Come on," Sean said, his hand still held out. "Let's see your real PDA."

underneath. All she wanted to do was rip the instrument off, throw it against the wall or onto the ground and stamp on it with her heel, twist and grind it into a thousand pieces that could be set on fire.

Exhausted, she leaned against the wall of a building and closed her eyes. She could almost hear her own voice pleading not to be fitted for the adult thanatometer she now wore.

"I don't wanna get a new one. It hurts. Why do I need a new one? I don't want it, and you can't make me get it," Sophia said, crossing her arms.

"Sophie, honey," her mum began, "you're fourteen and you have to get an adult thana. You've outgrown this one."

Sophia uncrossed her arms and turned to her mum. "Can't I just keep this one?" she said, holding out her arm. "Please. It's fine. See, it still fits."

"You said it hurt," her dad said.

Sophia crossed her arms again and, under her breath, said, "They all hurt."

"What was that?" her dad asked.

"They all hurt," Sophia yelled, "Every one of them, all the time and this new one won't be any better than this one or the one before or the one before that."

"Well, if they all hurt," her dad said, "it shouldn't matter if you get a new one because it'll all be the same."

Sophia turned her back to him and felt the urge to pull her hair out. "Easy for you to say when you're not the one getting it done."

"What did you say?" he asked.

Sophia turned. "I said that you're not the one who has to have this thing ripped off and then have a new one with bigger spikes stabbed into your wrist."

"None of my upgrades hurt, Soph. And your mother's never hurt. And nobody else's has ever hurt."

"Well mine do. And who are you going to believe, everybody else? Or me? What happened to you at your fittings or me at mine? I'm the one that feels it. Not you. And not anybody else."

"Oh, Jesus."

"Of course we believe you, Sophie," her mum said, taking hold of her hand. "It's just hard for us to understand when it never happened to us or anyone else, and the doctors say that it shouldn't hurt you."

"It's hard to believe you sometimes, Soph," her dad said.

"What?" Sophia said, yanking her hand away from her mother.

"Sean."

"You don't believe me. Is that it?" Sophia said to her dad before turning to her mum.

"It's not that, honey."

"Yes, it is. You don't believe me. You never have. You don't believe what my thana says and you don't believe me."

Sean and Lizette didn't respond.

"Fine, whatever. Let's just go," Sophia said, grabbing her coat from the closet.

"Honey …"

Sophia threw open the door and said, "I hope it hurts more than it ever has."

Sophia opened her eyes and focused on her thanatometer. She could feel the weight of it dragging down her arm and her entire body. Sophia sat on the ground, panting. Sweat dripped into her eyes, making them sting, so she shut them and began wiping away the sweat with her palms. She pictured herself at fourteen, sitting in the thanatometer-fitting chair in the examining room, avoiding eye contact with her mother. She remembered feeling glad that her father had decided to stay at home but also feeling angry with him for choosing to avoid seeing the pain she would have to endure.

Dr. Elliot Edwards entered carrying a small stainless steel box.

"Hello," he said, closing the door behind him. "Here for your final upgrade I see." He put the box down on the counter. "Time sure does fly doesn't it? Before you know it you'll be …"

"Twenty-seven," Sophia said, scowling at the floor.

"She's not too happy about being here, doctor," her mum said. "I practically had to drag her here."

"Oh. And why is that Sophia?"

Sophia sat still without answering.

"She says it hurts her."

"Is that so?" Dr. Edwards asked, taking the new thanatometer out of its box.

Sophia placed her arm on the armrest, which had a gap in it for her thanatometer, and then fastened the straps around her forearm and hand.

"They don't have to be quite so tight," the doctor said, sitting down beside Sophia with a shiny, black thanatometer in his hand.

It was identical to the one he wore, the latest model that Sophia's parents didn't even have yet.

He loosened the straps around Sophia's arm and said, "There. That's better isn't it?"

Sophia gazed at the new thanatometer and grew tense.

"Does your thanatometer hurt you?" Dr. Edwards asked.

"No."

"Did you tell your mother that it does?"

"I don't know."

The doctor placed the new thanatometer on the table beside him before moving closer to Sophia. "May I remove this one for you?"

When Sophia nodded, he placed his index and middle fingers under her wrist up against the straps, pressed down on her thanatometer's display with his thumbs, and peeled the straps back. Hundreds of tiny needlelike electrodes withdrew from Sophia's wrist, leaving countless minute red marks behind.

Sophia sat still and held back tears, her face twitching slightly from her pain. The doctor didn't notice her expression; he just pulled back the straps slowly and evenly, and when the thanatometer was finally removed from Sophia wrist, he said, "There you go," and dropped it into a trash can on the floor. He cleaned her wrist with some antiseptic swabs. "There is some slight irritation from the electrodes," he said. "Nothing to worry about."

Sophia sighed audibly. She felt euphoric and completely relaxed. The antiseptic was cold against her skin and almost tickled.

"Sophie, are you okay?" her mum asked.

"I thought you said it didn't hurt?" Dr. Edwards asked.

"It doesn't," Sophia said, closing her eyes and leaning back in the chair with a wide grin on her face.

The doctor grabbed the new thanatometer and brought it up to Sophia's wrist.

When the straps touched her, Sophia sat up, looked at him, and said, "Stop."

"Pardon me."

"Please. Could you wait before you put it on? Just for a minute or two. I like this feeling."

The doctor sat back and gazed at Sophia. "It actually feels differently with it on?" he asked. "You can feel a significant difference?"

"I feel like a different person."

Dr. Edwards shook his head and said, "That's impossible. You shouldn't feel anything. It must just be the shock of seeing the hairs on the thanatometer enter and exit your skin." He nodded authoritatively at Sophia's mother.

Sophia looked down at her red wrist and rubbed it with her left hand. She twisted her hand back and forth on her wrist for a moment before saying she was ready.

With a confused expression, the doctor slipped the new thanatometer onto Sophia's wrist.

As the imperceptibly larger electrodes pressed into her skin, Sophia looked down at her new thanatometer and saw the number twenty-seven displayed at the top of the screen. She began to cry. Wiping her tears away, she turned her gaze towards the wall and asked the doctor if he had any black tape.

Sophia looked down the street and noticed a thin string of smoke, the kind burning incense makes, escaping from a window at the base of a building across the street. She moved towards it and, when closer, saw a cobblestone staircase descending below street level. A large, red door with a knob directly in the center of it was at the base of the stairs. Sophia stepped down towards it. When she stood facing the door, she pushed the knob; the door creaked open, and a grey-haired woman appeared in the doorway, her face creased with age, her long, ratty hair spiraling onto her face and shoulders.

Sophia recoiled at the sight of the woman.

"Well, come in already," the old woman said. "No point stopping now when you've come so far." She disappeared into the home.

Sophia glanced back up the stairs and then stepped forward through the archway into the darkness of the home. She used the light spilling in through the open door to guide her as she waited for her eyes to adjust. Dust floated in the air around her face; it tickled her throat and made her want to cough. She cleared her throat and tried to fan the particles away, but the fanning just created more dust, so she stretched the collar of her shirt over her nose and breathed through the fabric. The dank stench of the house was masked by the smell of Sophia's own perspiration.

"Shut the door behind you, child," the old woman called out.

Sophia did as she was told. A moment after the door latched, she noticed the blue lights hanging from the ceiling.

"Care for a spot of this or that?"

"What?" Sophia asked. "I'm sorry?"

"I'll choose, I'll choose."

As Sophia moved towards the voice and the clang of pots and dishes, the blue lights grew brighter, and the stink in the house faded.

"Must have that. Too early for this."

Sophia removed her collar from her face and stepped into the kitchen. The air inside felt cold on her sweaty skin, giving her goosebumps.

A solid wood table and two chairs were in the corner of the cluttered kitchen. Pots and pans and cooking utensil hung on the walls, and packages of food filled the counters. As the short woman busied herself next to the stove, long beads, dangling around her waist clinked together every time she moved. The sound was rhythmic and somehow calming to Sophia.

"Take the one on the left, child," the woman said, glancing over her shoulder.

Sophia sat down at the table.

The woman turned and said, "Oh no, my left, my left."

Sophia quickly moved to the other chair; the old woman walked over and sat in the seat Sophia had vacated. She stared at Sophia, squinting and scratching her head. Sophia squirmed. She tried not to stare back at the woman but she couldn't help it.

"Zurie," the old woman said, placing her hand on her chest.

"Sophia."

Zurie continued to stare, and Sophia looked around for something to talk about. There was a picture of a young woman on top of the fridge.

"Is that your daughter?" Sophia asked.

Zurie glanced at the photo then back to Sophia, saying nothing.

"Your niece?"

Still, Zurie sat in silence, staring.

"An old picture of your mother? A close friend, an old neighbour, a stranger? Was the picture here when you moved in?"

"It's me," Zurie said.

"Oh," Sophia said. "You look very pretty."

The old woman reached her open palm out across the table towards Sophia and said, "Give me your arm child."

"What?" Sophia said, removing her arms from the table, and placing them in her lap. "Why?"

"Cuz, I wanna rip off that tape. See what's underneath," Zurie said, playing with her hair with her other hand.

Sophia leaned back in her chair; the wood dug into her shoulder blades. "How did you … No. Show me yours," she said.

Zurie slowly turned her wrist over on the table—it was bare. Sophia hadn't noticed before.

"Wait," Sophia said. "Where is it? Your other wrist, show me it too."

Zurie placed her left wrist up next to her right— both were bare.

"Where is it? Why don't you have one?"

"I did have a bracelet for a while but dropped it along the way," Zurie said. "Don't like the feel of things around my wrists."

Sophia raised her voice, "No, your thanatometer. Where is it?"

"Oh that. Dropped it along the way too."

The kettle began to beep. The woman got up and walked towards it. Sophia, mouth agape, watched the woman pour the steaming water into a black teapot.

The sound of the hot water cascading into the ceramic pot made Sophia realize how thirsty she was.

After placing the pot and two mugs in the centre of the table, Zurie sat back down across from Sophia and said, "Close your mouth, child. Tea will fill it soon enough."

"How is that possible?"

"Well, after it steeps, I'll pour you a mug."

"No, the thanatometer. How do you not have one?"

"Same reason yours has tape on it I 'spose."

"That's different. Mine's covered so my dad … so I don't think about it."

Zurie started pouring tea into the mugs. "Seems to be working," she said, chuckling.

Sophia stood up, and her chair fell backward. "It's not like that," she said.

"What's it like then?" Zurie asked, filling the second mug.

"You don't know anything," Sophia said, stepping towards the hall. "Nobody knows."

The woman stood up and flicked a light switch. A harsh glare illuminated the kitchen, accentuating Zurie's wrinkled face and matted hair.

The old woman put her wrist up in front of Sophia's face and said, "Nobody but me, child."

Countless tiny scars covered her entire wrist. Sophia's own wrist began to itch under the straps of her thanatometer—she wanted it off more than ever. Wanted to rip it from her and spill blood all over herself, the old woman, and the entire filthy kitchen.

Zurie lowered her arm and grabbed Sophia's wrist. Sophia jerked her arm back, trying to pull away from the old woman's calloused hands.

"Shh! It's okay, child."

Sophia stopped struggling. She was tired of hiding her thanatometer, and it didn't seem to matter if a crazy old woman, who she'd probably never see again, saw her PDA. She looked at the top of the woman's head, smelled the filth, marveled at the rat's nest, wondered when Zurie had last showered, and wanted a shower herself.

She felt the tape's adhesive cling to the glass face of her thanatometer as it was peeled off before being tossed to the ground. After staring at Sophia's bare thanatometer for a moment, Zurie looked up at her. Sophia gazed back at the woman for a moment, expecting to hear cries of disbelief or a cackle of ridicule, but the old woman said nothing.

Zurie turned and pulled Sophia by the arm deeper into the kitchen where she opened a drawer full of junk and rummaged through it, finally retrieving a roll of red tape. Zurie tore a piece off the roll with her teeth, stuck it to Sophia's thanatometer, patted Sophia's hand, and let go of her arm.

"Super adhesive," Zurie said. "It'll stay on as long as you want it to." Then the old woman turned off the light, sat back down, and took a sip of tea. "Your tea's getting cold, child."

Sophia, not knowing what to say or do, resumed her place on the opposite side of the table. She wrapped her hands around the warm mug in front of her, realizing how cold her hands were. The mug warmed her. She took a sip of tea and was warmed further.

Zurie smiled through rotted teeth and said, "It's good isn't it."

Sophia nodded, smiled back, and took another sip of tea.

THIRTEEN

With one hand clenched into a tight fist and the other gripping the phone, Sean Nolan paced across the length of his living room, shaking his head and mumbling to himself.

"I can't believe she ran away. Stupid. So stupid. What was she thinking?"

Sean resisted the urge to bury his fist into the wall—the most irrational impulse he had ever had—and smash the useless phone against the floor. There was nobody else to call. None of Sophia's friends or their friends had seen or heard from her, Rubin was already on his way, and Sophia wasn't calling. He squeezed the phone harder, hoping to break it or make it ring.

Sean just wanted Sophia to come home and apologize for running away but, for the first time since Sophia was born, he felt as if he had no control over his daughter and his helplessness infuriated him. Normally, he would have just worked out for a few hours to expel his anger, but he couldn't leave until Sophia returned. So he paced, with his desire to be destructive intensifying as he restrained it.

As Lizette sat on the couch watching her husband move back and forth across the room, she was reminded of the western gorilla she had seen at the city zoo. She had only taken Sophia there once over ten years before—Sophia didn't like the zoo because it made her sad to see all the animals in glass cages—but Lizette remembered the great ape pacing in front of the glass wall separating him from the countless people gawking, pointing, and knocking at him. The gorilla, ferocious and huge, appeared to want only one thing: to smash his glass prison and attack the people on the other side. Lizette saw that same impotent fury in Sean eyes. There was nothing he could do, and he knew it.

Even though Lizette just wanted Sophia to come home and didn't care where she'd been or what she'd done, she worried about Sean's reaction to their daughter's return and hoped Sophia would stay away long enough for him to fall asleep.

When the doorbell rang, Lizette hopped to her feet and raced to the door. She knew Sophia wouldn't ring the bell to her own house, but that didn't stop her from wishing to see, upon opening the door, her daughter standing on the welcome mat. Lizette felt dispirited when she saw Rubin instead of Sophia, but she also felt relieved that help had finally arrived.

"Thank you so much for coming, Rubin," she said, inviting him in.

Rubin stepped inside. Sean stood still in the living room, staring at Rubin. When Sean didn't speak or offer any gesture in response to his arrival, Rubin simply nodded to him and turned back to Lizette.

She was in the process of closing the door when Rubin said, "How are you two holding up?"

"Fine," Lizette said.

"Do you know where she is?" Sean asked from the other side of the room.

Rubin faced him. "Not yet," he said. "But I will soon enough."

"Aren't you supposed to be watching her twenty-four hours a day?"

"Sean," Lizette said, pleading with him to be civil.

"We're monitoring her vital signs," Rubin said, "not her whereabouts."

"Then how are you supposed to find her?"

"By looking for her, Sean," Rubin said. "Okay? I'm here to help. Now tell me what happened."

Sean didn't seem to hear the question; he pushed the talk button on the phone and began dialing.

"Who are you calling?" Lizette asked, wanting to take the phone away from him so that he couldn't call everyone they knew a second time and embarrass her further.

"I don't know," Sean yelled, hanging up the phone.

Lizette held out her hand and approached Sean. "Give me the phone," she said.

"Fine, take it," Sean said, handing it to her. "There's no point anyway."

Lizette took the phone and held it with both hands, trying to make it ring.

After a moment, Rubin moved into the living room and said, "Tell me what happened."

Sean began pacing again and didn't answer.

"She ran away after her race today," Lizette told Rubin.

"Why?"

Lizette sat back down on the couch and exhaled loudly. "Sean took the tape off today," she said.

"Oh, I see," Rubin said, suddenly angry with Sean.

He knew all along that Sean's stupid placebo effect wouldn't work. He had even observed it not working through his remote access to Sophia's thanatometer but had said nothing. Rubin regretted not speaking up. He assumed that Sophia was sneaking peeks at her thanatometer the entire time and would be unaffected by her thanatometer's constancy when Sean pulled off the tape. Rubin hadn't been worried about Sophia on his way over to the Nolan's but now he wanted to rush to his office, grab his tablet, and find her as fast as possible. Rubin didn't know if she was considering hurting herself, but if she was, he was the only one who could find and stop her.

"Her PDA hasn't changed," Sean said. "After all that training, it's the same. Not up. Not down. Exactly the goddamned same. We worked our asses off for years with nothing to show for it."

"Well, she won the race didn't she," Lizette said, becoming openly irritated with Sean.

"Big deal. Everyone competing is gonna out live her by a hundred years or more," Sean said, leaning closer to Lizette. "So who's the real winner, Liz? And who's the loser?"

Sean's face was close enough to slap, but Lizette turned away from him and tried to let the urge pass.

Rubin stepped towards the narrowing gap between Sean and Lizette, wary of overstepping his bounds, and said, "So neither of you knows where she might be?"

Sean stepped back and collapsed into a chair across from Lizette. He rubbed his face, shook his head, and said, "Nobody knows."

"What was the last thing she said, Sean?" Lizette asked, staring at the floor because she was still too angry to look at him.

"Nothing, she just freaked out and took off."

Lizette lifted her eyes towards Sean and said, "Well, what was the last thing you said to her? What made her run away? Did you tell her she was a loser? After she won the race, did you tell her that she was a loser, Sean?"

"Hey, she saw her PDA and took off, okay. You can't blame me for that," Sean said, his palms raised in front of him.

"She's only sixteen," Lizette yelled.

Rubin stepped in between them, obscuring their view of each other. "Calm down, both of you," he said. "Sit, breath, relax. Think of your own PDAs. She'll be back soon and all this worrying is just going to shorten your lives."

The room was silent for a moment as Sean and Lizette breathed deeply and tried to pacify themselves.

"Now," Rubin began, "where does she go when she's upset."

"Her room usually," Lizette said. "She's never run away like this."

"She probably just needed some time alone," Rubin said, looking at Lizette. He glanced at Sean who stared at the floor shaking his head.

"It didn't even move," Sean said. "Nothing." Sean looked up at Rubin. "Why? Why isn't it going up?"

"Give it a rest Sean," Lizette said.

"You know why," Rubin said. "And it won't change no matter how hard you try to make it." Rubin moved towards the front door; he had better things to do than counsel Sean. "I'll call the police department just in case. To see if they've picked up any young girls or had any reports of lone girls loitering around somewhere. But she probably just went to a friend's house. She'll come home when she's ready. Which will probably be right away, and I shouldn't be here when she does."

"But I called all her friends," Sean said.

"They could have lied for her," Lizette said.

"Exactly. Now, I have a few places that I can check and I'll call you when I find her," Rubin said, placing his hand on the doorknob.

Sean stood up and said, "Where are you going to look? I'll come with you."

Rubin opened the front door. "It's better if you're both here to greet her when she comes home. And don't be too hard on her when you see her," Rubin said. "She's been through enough today I'm sure."

Lizette stood and walked towards Rubin. She placed her hand on the door next to his. She wanted to hug him but couldn't in front of Sean. She also wanted to go with him and not to be left alone with her husband.

"Try not to worry," Rubin said to Lizette. "I'll call when I know where she is. And call me if you hear from her."

"I will," Lizette said.

Rubin turned and, as he made his way down the walkway leading to his car, he heard the door shut behind him. He stood beside his car for a moment, trying to remember the address of the building where Sophia's locator had shown her to be an hour before, but he couldn't. He knew he had to go back to his office and get his tablet in order to find her. Rubin took out his phone and dialed the police. When he lifted his head and the phone to his ear, he saw Sophia sitting on the lawn across the street. She sat staring at him, wearing shorts and a tank top with the large number twelve on her chest. Rubin, forgetting to breath for a few seconds, almost dropped his phone when he saw Sophia. Then he pretended not to notice her and got into his car. When the car door shut, he hung up his phone and gasped. He could feel her still looking at him, so he said, "Home," and the car drove away. Once down the street and around the corner, Rubin glanced into the rearview mirror and dialed the Nolan house. Lizette answered.

"Hi, it's Rubin. Sophia's sitting on your neighbour's lawn across the street."

"Oh my God. Really?

"Yes."

"Thank you so much."

"She saw me."

"Oh."

"You'll have to tell her something," Rubin said, trying to think of something plausible. "Tell her I was a detective who came to take down your statements."

"Okay. I will. Thanks again, Rubin."

"You're welcome," he said before hanging up.

He stared out the windshield, trying to ignore his heart pounding inside his chest and telling himself that Sophia didn't get a good look at his face.

"Cancel destination," he said. "Office."

Rubin needed his tablet. He needed to know where Sophia was at all times to ensure she never saw him again. He'd been careless, and it could never happen again.

FOURTEEN

At seven in the morning, Sophia had already been awake and staring at the ceiling for two hours. She couldn't remember the last time she slept past five. Even though her fifty-story apartment building was extremely quiet and her bedroom pitch dark, her internal alarm always went off just before five no matter what time she went to bed. At five, she would open the blinds and let the sunrise gradually light up her room while she gazed up at the ceiling.

She slept on a thin piece of foam on the floor with one blanket and a very small pillow. The only other things in her room were a lamp, her tablet, and a few clothes piled on the shelves in her closet. Her living room was even sparser: only a coffee table, which she ate at while sitting on the floor, with a little stereo on it was in the middle of the room.

At seven, Sophia reached for her tablet and checked her messages; she had two new ones. Another one from her mother, which she deleted without reading while wishing she'd stopped messaging her everyday, and one from Zack. Her finger hovered over the empty subject line of his message for a few seconds—she missed him a little or at least the feeling of him. Contemplating what she'd write back and conjuring nothing meaningful, she deleted his message without reading it.

Standing and tossing the tablet on her bed, she made her way into the kitchen wearing only panties and a thin T-shirt. She was hungry, but every dish she owned was in the sink with the dried remnants of past meals stuck to them. She had few dishes, which were usually dirty, so she routinely had to wash a couple to eat off. Always having a clean kitchen was the one thing she missed about living with her parents. Her mother had the ability, seemingly without effort, to keep a house constantly tidy; something Sophia didn't inherit. On the days when she just didn't have the nerve to wash dishes, Sophia would take a meal replacement pill and leave her apartment. But Sophia was out of pills so she loaded the dishwasher, started it, and by the time she had wiped the counters, the dishes were clean. As she filled the empty cupboards with the hot glassware, burning her fingers in the process, steam filled the kitchen. Sophia began to sweat.

She scarfed down a bowl of dry cereal and then filled her bowl again before moving towards the closed window in her living room, spooning more little flakes into her mouth as she did. She craved fresh air to cut through the humidity of her apartment and dry her sweat. As she extended her hand towards the windowpane, something streaked past the window heading straight down; Sophia only saw it for an instant but she knew what it was: a person wrapped in a blue and white sheet. Sophia dropped her bowl. It shattered against the floor. She swallowed hard and the partially chewed up cereal hurt her throat on the way down. Staring at the building across from her, its innumerable windows reflecting an image of her apartment building back at her, Sophia opened the window, stuck her head outside, and looked thirty stories down to the street below—a body lay sprawled and motionless on the concrete.

Sophia ran to her front door and tossed it open. Sprinting down the hallway, her heart pounding, her bare feet slapping against the ceramic tile, the balls of her feet and toes gripping and propelling her forward, she thought only about getting outside. She jumped into the elevator and rapidly hit the ground and close door buttons. As the elevator moved down, Sophia gripped the gap between the doors with her fingertips. When the doors dinged opened, Sophia helped pull the doors apart and then squeezed out of the elevator. She sprinted through the lobby towards the exit. A man stood inside the foyer on his cell phone. Sophia ran past him and tossed open the front door, slowing to a walk once outside and looking down at the body.

"I just called," the man said, sticking his head outside the foyer. "They're on their way."

Sophia ignored him and stepped across the rough concrete. She breathed heavily through her mouth and wasn't blinking. A woman's lifeless body, partially draped in a white and blue striped housecoat, lay twisted and broken facedown in a pool of blood. Her left leg and arm were hyperextended with bones protruding through her skin. Sophia bent down and took hold of the closest corner of the robe. She pulled it down to cover the woman's exposed panties, legs, and lower back.

"Don't touch her," the cell phone man yelled from inside the building.

Sophia glanced over her shoulder at him; he shook his head, his eyes wide and ugly with fear. She turned away and, still holding the corner of the robe, slid the soft fleece down until it rested just above the woman's ankles. Then she stepped towards the woman's head and glanced up at the entrance to the building across from her. Three people stood like statues in the lobby. They gawked at Sophia, but she turned her back on them and squatted down.

The woman's long brown hair was damp and covered her face. As Sophia extended her finger to brush the hair back, she wondered why it was wet, if the woman had showered before jumping, if she was soaked in sweat. Sophia slid a clump of hair back behind the woman's ear, revealing a soft, flushed cheek. She kept pushing hair back until her fingers were wet and the woman's profile was exposed. Sophia smelled her fingers; they smelt like her mother's shampoo—sweet botanicals and soothing herbs—and for a second she remembered sitting between her mother's legs getting her hair blow dried, her mother's long hair draped over her, the herbal shampoo scent the only thing she could smell.

Then Sophia thought the dead woman looked like her mother, but she quickly pushed the thought out of her mind and pushed more of the woman's hair out of her face. Her eyes were shut and the side of her face towards the ground rested against broken and bloodied hands. On the woman's right wrist, her thanatometer was blinking. Sophia looked closer at the display.

PDA 121.3

Age 47

bpm 172

Systolic: 170 mmHg

Diastolic: 120 mmHg

38.5 °C (101.3 °F)

As Sophia read the thanatometer, it stopped flashing and went blank. Time seemed to stop. Sophia felt as if she were under water, holding her breath so she wouldn't drown, unable to hear anything until the wailing of sirens was directly behind her. She stood and turned to see two police cars, an ambulance, and a fire truck. One of the cops and paramedics jumped out of their vehicles and ran toward her.

"Hey. What are you doing? Get away from there," the paramedic said.

Sophia stayed still. "I think she jumped," she managed to say. "I saw—"

"Move," the paramedic said, stepping between Sophia and the body.

Sophia stumbled back and watched him work. He grabbed the woman's limp wrist with his latex-gloved hands and inspected her thanatometer. Pushing a button on the side of the display, the screen flashed to life but again went blank and lifeless when he released the button. When he dropped the woman's wrist, her arm slapping against the ground with a dull thud, he waved over the other paramedic.

"I saw her fall," Sophia began. "It was from some floor above me."

A tall male police officer in a freshly pressed navy blue uniform stepped in front of her. Sophia's eyes moved up to meet his.

"Why are you dressed like that? Where are your clothes, ma'am?" the cop asked, his hands on his cluttered utility belt, his short, spiky hair moving forward slightly as he raised his eyebrows.

"What? I don't know," Sophia said, realizing she was practically naked. She stretched her shirt down over her panties and crossed her arm.

"Is this your building here?" the cop said, pointing to her building.

Sophia glanced over and said, "Yeah, but she jumped. I saw her from my—"

"It'd be best," he said with his palms held up and facing Sophia, "if you just went back to your apartment and put some clothes on, ma'am. Okay?"

The cop turned his attention to the man in the foyer and yelled, "Go back to your apartment, sir," while reaching around Sophia and putting his hand on her back. He turned her away from the body.

A female cop approached from behind. The cop guiding Sophia turned, pointed to the crowd that had gathered in the lobby across the street, and said, "Get those people in that building over there to return to their homes."

As the female cop trotted away holding her belt, another paramedic arrived pushing a gurney. The two paramedics lifted the woman face up onto the gurney and covered her with a white sheet. Two firefighters, covered from head to toe in yellow uniforms, exited the fire truck and began pulling hoses from one of the truck's side compartments.

Sophia, looking back and trying to watch what was happening, was led away by the cop.

"Come on. Let's go," the cop said as he began stepping more briskly, his hand pushing harder into Sophia's back.

"Wait a sec," Sophia said, spinning around to face the cop and slapping his hand away. "Don't you want to know what happened?" she asked. "I saw her."

"We know everything there is to know from the phone call, ma'am."

"But did that guy see it? Does he even know?"

The cop opened the building door for Sophia and said, "Forget about it. It's not your concern."

"If not mine then whose? Yours? You don't even fucking care."

The cop took a step towards Sophia, staring in her eyes. "Go to your home, ma'am," he said, his chest pushed out. "Or I'll have to arrest you for indecent exposure."

Sophia scoffed but stepped backward through the open door and entered the lobby. The cop shut the door, turned his back on Sophia, and began talking into the radio mic on his shoulder. She looked past the cop to see the woman being wheeled away on the gurney. Sophia then walked back to the elevator, breathing heavy, clenching her teeth and fists. There was a small bench against one of the walls that she wanted to pick up and toss through the closest window. At the closed elevator doors, she glanced back at the cop, who stood guarding the apartment entrance. When the elevator doors opened, there was a couple in their seventies inside. They stepped forward to exit the elevator but then saw Sophia standing there in her panties and T-shirt and the emergency vehicles outside, and stepped back deeper into the elevator.

Sophia watched them and said, "Where are you going?"

The elevator doors began to close and Sophia forced them open again.

"Don't you wanna see what's going on?"

The couple shook their heads, and the man said, "We were just …"

"Running away," Sophia said. "Fine, go ahead. Go to your *home*. Nothing to see here. Nothing to see here."

She let the elevator doors shut and looked back outside. The gurney was almost at the ambulance; Sophia couldn't let them take her away without somebody knowing the truth, so she sprinted through the lobby, shoved open the foyer door—hitting the cop in the back with it and making him stumble forward— and ran to the gurney. Sophia threw back the white sheet covering the woman, grabbed hold of both sides of the gurney, and pressed herself into the limp body.

"She jumped," Sophia yelled, her face against the woman's chest, blood smearing across her cheek. "I saw her jump."

The paramedics tried to pull Sophia away, but she held firm to the gurney. When they began prying her fingers from the metal one by one, Sophia grabbed hold of other parts of the gurney. She couldn't be removed until the cop grabbed her from behind and yanked her back away while each paramedic loosened her grip. With Sophia hoisted into the air, the paramedics quickly covered the woman up again and made for the ambulance.

"Let me go," Sophia screamed, struggling.

As the cop carried her towards the squad car, the two firefighters switched on a pump that drowned out Sophia's cries. The firefighters extended two pressure sprayers towards the spot where the body had impacted. Sophia tried to kick one of the firefighters when they passed her but missed.

They began spraying. Within seconds all the red was washed into the gutter and forced down the drain, the woman was loaded into the ambulance, Sophia pressed against a squad car, and one of the paramedics ran over and stuck a needle into her arm.

Sophia felt a prick in her shoulder and yelled for them to get away from her but her voice was inaudible next to the noise of the pressure washers. Then she could no longer speak and her eyes could no longer focus. Her strength began to leave her as another car screeched to a halt directly beside the police cars, and a man ran toward her. Sophia couldn't see his face, but she felt his arms wrap around her and take her from the police officers. At that moment, in the arms of a stranger, she went limp and lost consciousness.

FIFTEEN

Rubin was sitting inside his car two blocks away from Sophia's apartment building when the body of a woman smashed into the sidewalk; she bounced slightly before lying still on the concrete.

Rubin jolted and covered his open mouth with his hands. He couldn't believe what he had just seen. He looked up at the building and searched for an open window, but, finding none, turned back to the motionless body.

"Sophia," he said, suddenly even more terrified.

He grabbed his tablet and frantically tried to open the remote access to Sophia's thanatometer as fast as he could, but his shaking hands slowed him down. As Rubin struggled to connect to Sophia's thanatometer, he prayed that it wasn't her lying dead on the sidewalk. He was there to keep her safe, even from herself if he had to. Rubin logged into Sophia's thanatometer—her heart was still beating, a little faster than normal, but she was alive.

Rubin let his head fall back against the headrest and tried to slow his heart by putting his hand over it. As his heart pounded into his palm, Rubin felt ashamed to have assumed that Sophia had actually killed herself.

Still, she was almost twenty-seven and hadn't been for a checkup in over six years, which caused him, for the past year, to start following her for a few hours everyday. Rubin looked back at the body lying on the ground; he knew that Sophia could have killed herself a long time ago if she had wanted to and that she didn't need him to stop her.

After he had calmed down, Rubin called the police. When he knew the authorities were on the way, he turned his attention to the tablet and opened the locator tab beneath Sophia's thanatometer readout; she was on the ground floor of her building, moving toward the body. Rubin looked up from his tablet and saw Sophia run outside wearing only underwear and a T-shirt. He watched her examine and cover up the lifeless woman. He wanted to go to her, wrap clothes around her, and take her back upstairs before the police showed up, but he couldn't. She had no idea who he was. He'd be the same as a cop in her eyes.

When the emergency vehicles showed up and the police officer began ushering Sophia back into the building, Rubin felt relieved. He rubbed his face and eyes for a minute before looking at his tablet again. Sophia moved deeper into the building for a moment but then seemed to be running back towards the body.

He looked up and saw her knock over the officer before hurrying to the gurney. She threw off the sheet and hugged the body. Then the officer she'd struck grabbed her from behind, lifted her into the air, and hauled her to his squad car. Rubin started his car and sped towards Sophia. He screeched to a halt beside the police cruiser and, jumping out of his car, saw a paramedic pull a needle from Sophia's arm. He ran to her.

"I'm Rubin Russell with National Wellness," he yelled, trying to speak over the pressure sprayers of the firefighters who had already started cleaning up the blood.

The police officer's expression became even sterner when he looked at Rubin, so Rubin presented his National Wellness ID badge. The officer relaxed.

Rubin leaned into the officer and yelled, "This woman is under my care," into his ear.

"Sorry, sir," the officer yelled back. "We didn't know."

"Forget about it," Rubin said, placing his arms around Sophia's limp body. "I'm taking her back upstairs. You just worry about cleaning up this mess."

The officer nodded and lowered Sophia into Rubin's arms.

Rubin carried her to the building, and the officer hurried forward to hold the door open for him. He nodded to the officer, made his way through the lobby, and entered the elevator.

Rubin laid Sophia down in her bed. He could hear the racket from the pressure sprayers through the open window in the living room, so he shut it. Sophia's apartment became silent, and Rubin's ears started to ring. He felt something crunch beneath the soles of his shoes and looked down—he stood on shards of broken glass and flakes of crushed cereal. He cleaned up the mess and checked on Sophia. She was sleeping with her head askew, reminding Rubin of how she looked as a baby in the hospital nursery.

Rubin stood beside the bed and leaned down to brush the hair off her face. Noticing the blood on her cheek, he rushed to the kitchen and wet a rag. After he'd wiped the blood away, he kissed her forehead. *Open your eyes*, he thought, wanting Sophia to see him so he would have to tell her who he was. But Sophia didn't stir. Rubin stood up straight and gazed down at her. She looked just like her mother. He had seen the similarities in the photographs he'd taken but, standing a few feet from her, Sophia could have been Lizette at twenty-six.

Rubin pressed his index finger into Sophia's hand. He wanted her to squeeze it the way she had the first day they met, but she didn't.

"Take care of yourself, Sophia" Rubin said, putting his hands and the damp, bloody rag in his pockets. "I'll be here if you need me."

Rubin quietly left her apartment and shut the door quickly behind him. By the time he stepped outside the lobby doors on the ground floor, the emergency vehicles were gone and every trace of the woman's death had been washed away. Rubin stared at the wet concrete; it dried quickly in the summer sun. Soon the woman's death would only be a memory. He didn't know if Sophia would think she had dreamt it or not, but he hoped she would.

Rubin stepped around the evaporating wet spot, got into his car, and drove away.

SIXTEEN

Five hours later, Sophia woke up in her own bed, mind and eyes heavy with sleep. She hadn't dreamt, or at least she couldn't remember dreaming. She rolled over onto her side and felt a dull ache in her shoulder. At first she didn't know why it hurt but then she remembered the paramedic stabbing her in the arm with a needle. Sophia jumped out of bed and hurried to the living room window; she opened it, stuck her head outside, and looked down—the woman's body was gone. Sophia brought her head back inside her apartment and noticed that the shattered bowl of cereal, which she should have been standing on, was also gone.

"It couldn't have been a dream," she said, shaking her head.

She felt the ache in her arm again and rushed to the bathroom. Lifting her short sleeve, she examined her arm in the mirror and saw a tiny, red puncture wound.

She held her sore shoulder with her hand and said, "I knew it."

Trying to recall what happened, Sophia paced across her kitchen. She remembered being carried towards the cop car right before blacking out but she couldn't remember how she had gotten back into her bed. The thought of the cop carrying her into her apartment filled her with loathing. She looked for his footprints but found none. Then she looked inside the trash can and found cereal mixed with pieces of broken bowl. Sophia didn't think the cop would have clean up her mess but she knew she hadn't either. She had the vague memory of a man approaching her right before she blacked out while in the cop's arms but she couldn't recall the man's face.

Suddenly, the dead woman was all Sophia could think about. Her limp body lying on the cold concrete, the blood stretching out beneath her. Sophia wondered what floor the woman lived on, if she had family or lived alone. Had she seen the woman before in the elevator or the lobby or the pool? Had she held the front door open for her once and exchanged smiles with her? Would anyone miss her? Would anyone miss me?

Sophia had always ignored her neighbours and shared a mutual disregard with all of them. It was the way she liked it, until now. She hadn't known her dead neighbour but she would never forget her. She wanted to have a wake for her. She wanted to knock on every door in the building and introduce herself to everyone and invite them all onto the roof to mourn their neighbour who had jumped to her death. She'd show them all her thanatometer. She'd tell them they should all meet on the roof again to see what happens to her on her birthday.

Sophia didn't want to be wheeled away to an ambulance, nobody around, her blood being washed into the sewer. She looked down at her thanatometer, at the red tape covering the display. She hadn't seen her PDA in years. She pretended it didn't exist and that it didn't matter even if it did exist. But, if she were honest with herself, Sophia was afraid of her thanatometer, and that fear infuriated her.

Scratching at the tape, she felt restless and started pacing again. As she moved back and forth across the length of her apartment, her energy intensified and spiked, making her want to scream or run as fast as she could across the city. Dropping to the floor, Sophia started doing pushups, exhaling loudly when straightening her arms and inhaling through clenched teeth when nearing the floor; she stared at her thanatometer the entire time. Her hair fell in her face as she pushed up and dropped down, her breath quickening, her heart pounding faster. She never wanted to stop. People began drifting in and out of her mind—her father, the cop, her mother, the dead woman, the paramedics, the people in rubber suits, the man who'd touched her just as she'd blacked out, Zack. Sophia exhaled louder, harder, bearing her teeth every time she pushed up. At fifty, she jumped to her feet and paced again, her muscles swelling with strength and vigor.

Sophia grabbed an elastic from a drawer and tied her hair back tightly. As she brought her arms back down to her sides, the red tape on her thanatometer caught her eye. She looked at it for a few seconds before picking at one of the corners and ripping it off; the glue peeled from the glass with a high-pitched squeal as it exposed her thanatometer's display.

Sophia smushed the tape between her hands, marched towards the window, and tossed the crumpled piece of red outside. She watched for a moment as it floated down. When she lost sight of it, she smiled and felt free. Then she turned back to her thanatometer: her predicted death age was still twenty-seven, and she only had three months to live. Sophia closed her eyes. She felt healthy and wasn't ready to die. But if she only had three months left, she was going to live more in a quarter of a year than she had in twenty-six years. She wanted to do something. To affect people. To be remembered, but she didn't know how and she didn't know what.

Sophia thought of the old woman she'd met when she was sixteen, Zurie. She was the only person Sophia had willfully shown her thanatometer to. The only person who hadn't tried to explain it or change it. The only person who hadn't judged her.

Sophia dressed quickly and left her apartment. She needed to see Zurie again. She just hoped that she could remember the way to that red door.

SEVENTEEN

Out of breath, Sophia knocked on Zurie's red door. She had run all the way there, her legs remembering the way. The door opened a crack, and the hunched, old woman peeked her wrinkled face out into the sunlight; she squinted at the glare of the sun and appeared to have just woken up.

"She jumped," Sophia blurted out as soon as she saw Zurie's face. "And they just picked her up and tossed her into the back of an ambulance. They didn't care who she was or what happened."

Sweat streamed down Sophia's face like tears. She wanted to see the anger she felt reflected in the old woman's face, but Zurie's expression didn't change; she simply nodded and stepped back into the darkness of her home, leaving the door open.

Sophia regretted going there. Zurie didn't care. Nobody did. But she had nowhere else to go so she stepped inside and slammed the door behind her. Because of how bright it was outside, she couldn't see anything in the dark home, which made her even angrier.

"Come on," she said, squeezing her eyes shut and opening them over and over again.

Sophia faced the door with her fists pressed up against it. She wanted to punch through and splinter the wood. She craved cuts and broken bones, hands that ached from swelling and dripped with blood. Pain was better than anger, better than feeling trapped.

"Slam it again, child," Zurie said from the darkness.

Sophia turned towards the old woman's voice but could only see her silhouette against the dim light of the kitchen. "What?"

"Slam it."

Sophia opened and slammed the door with less force than she had the first time.

"Again," Zurie said.

She opened the door and slammed it harder.

"Again."

And harder.

"Again."

And harder.

"Again."

And harder and faster until the old woman, no longer having to prompt Sophia, stood silently in the dark while Sophia continued to slam the door, groaning and gasping for breath as she did so. The hinges squeaked as the door crashed into its frame and waited for the next slam, which started to come more slowly and with less force.

Exhausted, Sophia's rage disappeared. She slammed the door weakly one last time and then sat down and leaned against it. Sitting there on the cold floor, her back touching the hard wood, Sophia became consumed with thoughts of her own death. She began to cry, her tears dripping onto her sweat-soaked shirt. She trembled uncontrollably and brought her knees to her chest, hugging them to try and calm herself. Unable to, she slapped herself in the face, barely feeling any pain.

"That's enough," Zurie said, standing above Sophia and looking down at her.

Sophia looked up into the old woman's eyes and smacked herself again.

"Enough," Zurie cried.

Sophia lay down onto the floor, and continued to sob. Lying on her side, she hugged herself and began to wail. She couldn't hold back and she didn't want to. Her cries echoed in the hall and her tears fell to the dusty ground.

Eventually, her sobs turned to whimpers, her trembling to stillness, and her tears to streaks of dried salt down her face. Sophia heard Zurie slurping something in another room, so she sat up and looked down the hall to the kitchen. When she stood up, her legs felt weak and her knees shook as she made her way towards the kitchen.

Zurie was seated at her table sipping tea. The chair opposite her was pulled out with an empty mug on the table in front of it. A teapot was in the center of the table.

Sophia sat down and looked at the mug in front of her.

"Help yourself, child," Zurie said.

Sophia reached for the teapot and could barely lift it; as she filled her mug, her hand shook with the effort. After one sip, she felt better. The anger was gone; she had slammed it all out. The fear was gone; her tears had washed it away. She took another sip, thinking only about the tea nourishing her.

"So you saw them get rid of somebody did you?" Zurie asked. "Some woman?"

Sophia nodded and stared into her cup as she took another sip.

"You could have stopped her, you know. If you'd known her, if you'd loved her ... you could have stopped her."

Sophia put her cup down on the table and said, "But I …"

"But you weren't meant to, child," Zurie said, taking a sip of tea.

"But how do you know?" Sophia asked.

"If you were, you would have."

"But how do you know that?"

"Because it happened."

Sophia took a deep breath and, when she exhaled, felt lightheaded. She looked down at her thanatometer, held it up to Zurie, and said, "She jumped because of this didn't she?"

"Yes."

"How many more like her?"

Zurie shrugged and said, "Lots more like her. More every day."

Sophia closed her eyes. She pictured herself standing above the woman's lifeless body lying twisted and torn on the concrete. Then she looked up and saw a multitude of people plummeting down towards her; each of them wearing the same bathrobe as the dead woman on the ground. As the bodies rapidly tumbled down towards her, Sophia crouched and covered her head.

Sophia opened her eyes. Zurie was staring at her. "I have to do something," she said. "But I don't know what."

Zurie reached into her dress pocket and pulled out a pipe and a lighter. She held the flame over the end of the pipe and started puffing.

"What is that?" Sophia asked, her eyes widening.

Zurie extinguish the lighter, exhaled smoke, and said, "Tobacco."

"What does it do?"

"It helps you think."

Zurie took a puff, coughed, and then held the pipe out to Sophia.

"Is it bad for you?" Sophia asked, hesitating.

"What? You afraid it'll shorten your life?" Zurie said, waving the pipe in the air. "Take some, child. Live for the moment."

Sophia took the pipe and inhaled. She coughed as the smoke entered her lungs. Holding the pipe out to Zurie, Sophia felt as if she was about to breath fire, her face turning red, her lungs burned.

Zurie cackled and pushed the pipe back towards Sophia. When Sophia stopped choking, her eyes full of water, she took another puff and coughed less and another and another until she didn't cough at all. She offered the pipe to Zurie again, and the old woman smiled wide enough to show all of her rotten teeth.

"Thinking better now?" Zurie asked, taking the pipe.

Sophia coughed a little and said, "I don't think so."

"You must make people listen to you," she said, taking a puff.

"What should I say?"

"Say?" Zurie shook her head. "Don't say. Do. They'll listen to what you do," she said. Then she held out her wrist and showed off the scars that had replaced her thanatometer. "Show them this."

Sophia examined the tiny scars and thought about how much it must have hurt when Zurie pulled off her thanatometer; the skin ripping and tearing as the electrodes were yanked towards the open air, blood covering her wrist and running down her arm. She thought of her own wrist and all the electrodes evading it. She rolled her wrist around and could feel the metal moving beneath her skin. She wanted them out of her. Wanted the blood, the scars.

Everybody needs them out, Sophia thought, reaching for the pipe. *Everybody needs scars.*

EIGHTEEN

At midnight, Sophia stood beneath a lamppost at the edge of her grandfather's property. The house, along with the walkway leading to it, was lit up by numerous lights. It appeared somehow smaller than Sophia remembered.

Eight years had passed since she'd seen her grandpa. As she strode up the path towards the house, Sophia recalled her first memory of the old man.

She was two or three and holding her mother's hand as she walked slowly up the walkway. Reaching the steps, Lizette lifted Sophia into her arms and carried her to the front door.

Sophia saw a brass door knocker in the shape of a lion's head in the centre of the door and grabbed it; her mother helped her knock it into the door.

An old man opened the door. He wore a black suit, a white shirt, and a red tie. Sophia stared at the tie for a long time before she heard her name and looked up at her grandpa's wrinkled face —his eyebrows were grey and bushy, his nose was big, and he didn't seem to have lips. Sophia hid from him, burrowing into her mum's shoulder.

"Nice to meet you Sophia," he said, his voice gruff. "There's no need to hide your face from me, child. I'm your grandfather."

"It's okay, honey," her mother said. *"Say hello to your grandpa."*

Sophia peeked at the old man. She didn't speak but she also didn't turn away again. He smiled and held out his hand to her. When Sophia didn't take it, his smile faded, and his hand dropped back down to his side.

Sophia climbed the steps and came face to face with the lion-head door knocker. She petted the lion's nose a few times before reaching for the security screen beside the front door. The screen illuminated when she touched it, displaying a numeric pad. Sophia had watched her mother and father enter the access code many times but she had never entered it herself. Worried that the code had been changed since she had last been there, she keyed in her grandpa's year of birth. When the lock unbolted, Sophia stepped inside, leaving the door open a crack so that she could leave in a hurry if she had to.

The house nauseated her. It always had. It was immaculately clean and smelt of antiseptic, which reminded Sophia of a hospital.

Standing at the base of the winding stairs leading to the upper floor, Sophia listened for the on duty nurse. Hearing nothing, she looked into the dining room and saw the large table she used to draw under—it had been her only safe place in the whole house. Turning to the living room, she saw her grandpa's old chair. He had always been in that chair, his thanatometer hooked up to something while a nurse monitored him, but now the chair was empty and the living room dark.

Sophia climbed the stairs. On the second floor, she could see her grandfather's bedroom door at the end of the long hall. An antique church pew was beside the staircase facing his door. Sophia touched the closest armrest of the old wooden bench; she remembered the last time she had sat there.

"I'm not going in," Sophia said to her mum, crossing her arms. *"He creeps me out."*

They stood in the hall outside of her grandpa's bedroom.

"Keep your voice down and show some respect, Sophia," Lizette said, scowling, her voice a harsh whisper. *"He's your grandfather. Anyone else would be privileged to have him in their family."*

Sophia drew back; she had been scolded by her mother before but had never heard such disgust and exasperation in her voice.

"Do you know how far some of those people out there have traveled just to come see him?" Lizette asked, pointing outside to the people lined up down the walkway. *"Strangers that are grateful for just two minutes of his time?"*

"Okay. I'm sorry," Sophia said, shrinking away from her mother. "What's with you?"

Lizette put her hands over her face and sighed. "Nothing," she said. "I'm just," she looked at Sophia, "... tired of the way you talk about him." She brushed the hair off of Sophia's face and said, "I'm sorry. I didn't mean to yell at you but I've just never heard you say anything nice about him."

Sophia turned away; seeing disappointment in her mother's eyes made her feel like a bad person.

"He means a lot to a lot of people you know," Lizette said.

Sophia nodded, more as an apology to her mother than acquiescence to her opinion, but she knew her mum would assume both. She didn't care how her mum interpreted her nod as long as she was forgiven.

Lizette reached for the golden doorknob and turned it—the door opened a crack.

"Just wait out here until I'm finished," she said. "Or come in if you change your mind. I'm sure he'd love to see you."

As Lizette swung the door open and stepped inside, Sophia saw her grandpa propped up in bed, surrounded by computers, an oxygen mask over his mouth and nose, a nurse tending to a glowing cable attached to his thanatometer.

In the moment before her mum shut the door, Sophia made eye contact with her grandpa. He appeared as displeased with her as her mother was. Then the door shut, and Sophia was alone in the hall. She sat down on the pew beside the stairs and waited. After a few minutes, a woman in her sixties climbed the stairs and sat beside Sophia.

The woman smiled and said, "Have you been waiting long to see Dr. Léon Rousseau?"

"I'm not um, he's my grandfather."

The woman became excited. She took Sophia's hands in hers and said, "You are blessed. Truly blessed. How old are you, dear?"

"Eighteen," Sophia said, shying away from the woman.

She bowed her head and said, "It is an honour to meet you."

Sophia gaped at the top of the woman's head and then glanced at the closed bedroom door to see if her mother was coming out; she wasn't.

When the woman lifted her head, Sophia gently pulled her hands away.

"I gotta go," she said, standing up.

"Before you leave, may I see your death age," the woman said, gesturing to Sophia's right wrist.

Under her long sleeve, Sophia's thanatometer had the red piece of tape on it, but Sophia still felt the need to put her hands behind her back to hide it.

"Perhaps one day people will be coming here to see you," she said.

"I don't think so."

"So modest," the woman said, holding out her hand. "Show me your PDA, dear."

"I have to go," Sophia said, turning her back on the woman.

She moved towards the bedroom door. It opened, and her mum emerged. Sophia saw her grandpa again but this time he sat in a chair in the middle of the room, dressed in one of his suits, and fiddling with the tablet on his lap. He was unattached to any computer or respiratory machine. In fact, the room was completely void of any hospital equipment.

Sophia frantically searched the bedroom with her eyes.

"Is everything okay?" Lizette asked, pulling the door closed behind her.

"Fine," Sophia said, watching the door latch shut.

"Okay. Let's go."

As Sophia walked past the woman waiting on the pew, she pretended not to notice her wave goodbye.

Sophia took her hand from the pew and looked down the hallway at her grandfather's bedroom door. She regretted not going in to see him eight years before and never visiting him. Approaching the door, she wondered how much he had deteriorated over the years. As she turned the doorknob, she just hoped he could still speak.

Inside the bedroom, Sophia shut the door and fell back against it. Where his bed had been, her grandfather, wearing a black body suit, floated in the centre of a four-sided glass tank full of liquid and surrounded by computers. His eyes were closed and his mouth and nose were covered with an oxygen mask. In front of the tank, a large screen displayed his thanatometer readout:

PDA 152.5

Age 146.2

bpm 65

Systolic: 140 mmHg

Diastolic: 90 mmHg

37.0 °C (98.6 °F)

Watching him float lifelessly in his glass prison, Sophia slowly walked towards the tank and placed her palms against the glass. Up close, he looked dead. But he wasn't. Not even death could touch him inside that tank. Sophia started to cry.

"You want to live six more years like this?"

She closed her eyes and let her forehead rest against the glass. She imagined taking her grandfather's place. Her skin pruned, her hair thin and white, her mouth covered by an oxygen mask that forced air into her lungs. She was helpless, unable to die and unable to live. When she opened her eyes, the tank ceased to be her grandfather's prison. It was his body that trapped him there.

Sophia pushed away from the tank. "I'm gonna get you out," she said, turning and looking for something to throw.

Sophia grabbed the wires plugged into the back of the screen in front of the tank and yanked them out. Then she lifted the thirty-inch monitor up above her head and turned back to the tank.

NINETEEN

Rubin sat in his car across the street from Dr. Léon Rousseau's house. He had followed Sophia's locator there after noticing that the sedative had worn off and she had left her apartment. He didn't know what she was doing at her grandfather's house; he just wanted her back in her bed where he knew she was safe. He could have drugged her himself if he had to. Rendered her unconscious and taken her home or to the hospital. He could have quarantined her in a hospital room with twenty-four-hour surveillance until her twenty-seventh birthday. *It would make Tabitha happy. It would make everything easier too, and I could actually get some sleep.*

Rubin's PDA had fallen in the last year and his constant worry of Sophia kept him from sleeping through the night. Occasionally he'd muse about dying of sleep deprivation. Driving home in the dark he constantly saw things that weren't really there running out in front of his car. Sometimes he'd swerve only to realizes that he'd maneuvered to avoid hitting a hallucination.

Waiting for Sophia to emerge from her grandfather's house, Rubin stared down at his tablet, which displayed Sophia's locator in the top corner of the screen—showing her on the second floor of the house—and a file on the woman who had jumped to her death on the rest of the screen. Rubin scrolled through the dead woman's life. Victoria Bachman, 47. She had increased her initial PDA by seven years, had two teenaged sons, and a fifteen-year marriage. She'd never seen a psychologist, appeared to be healthy, both physically and emotionally, and, just like most suicides, she seemed to have no reason to kill herself. There was a picture of the woman attached to her file—she smiled broadly, dimples on her cheeks, her long, cocoa-coloured hair hanging over her shoulders, something in her green eyes making her seem kind. She was happy, attractive, normal. She looked like Claudia.

Rubin quickly closed Victoria's file; he didn't want to think of her anymore or his ex-wife, so he maximized Sophia's locator. She was still on the second floor.

"What are you doing here Sophia?" he said, turning to the house.

She'd just witnessed a suicide, been drugged by the authorities, almost arrested, and then had regained consciousness in her own bed only to go visit her grandfather after midnight. The whole thing made Rubin uneasy. He got out of his car and made his way towards the house. When he climbed the steps, Rubin saw that the door was open.

She knows I'm following her, he thought. *And she left the door open for me.*

Glancing back at his car before pushing his way inside, Rubin made sure not to latch the door when he closed it behind him.

Rubin stood in the entranceway; the house was extremely quiet. It appeared that either no one was home or else everyone was asleep. Then Rubin heard glass shatter from somewhere upstairs.

"Sophia," he gasped, unable to move for a moment, the sounds of splintering glass paralyzing him.

The next sounds Rubin heard, a loud thump and Sophia's scream, jolted him out of his paralysis. He ran up the stairs and stopped on the second floor, searching beneath the closed doors for lights on inside. When he saw light coming from the room at the end of the hall, he ran towards it and, without slowing down, put his shoulder into the closed door.

TWENTY

Sophia smashed the computer screen into the front of the tank, shattering a glass pane. Synthetic amniotic fluid mixed with broken glass poured out of the tank and down onto Sophia. As shards sliced into her arm and cheek, Sophia jumped back, dropped the screen onto the floor, covered her face, and cried out in pain. Then her grandfather's limp body flopped onto the floor, colliding with her legs and making her fall backwards; the back of her head hitting the floor.

Dazed, covered in slime, bleeding, Sophia lay still beneath the dead weight of her grandfather. When she heard him gasping beneath his oxygen mask, Sophia sat up and looked at him; he tried to open his eyes but couldn't because of the thick slime coating them. She cradled him in her arms and quickly removed the mask. He inhaled, his lungs making a tired wheezing sound, and then he began to cough. Sophia placed a hand on his chest; his coughing quickly subsided. She cleaned the slime from his eyes with her fingers; he opened them and stared up at Sophia. The anger and fear she saw in his wild, green eyes made her feel as if she were a child again, timid and scared, so she turned away.

You did the right thing, she thought, gazing at the bedroom door and wanting to run away, sensing the old man's eyes on her. *He needed out.*

Sophia turned back to the shriveled old man in her arms and looked into the eyes she had always avoided as a child. There was nothing terrifying about him; he was a sad, weak, dying old man. Sophia's fear became pity as she cleaned the fluid from the rest of his face.

"You," he said, his voice a raspy whisper.

"That's right. It's me. Sophia. Your granddaughter."

"You ... killed me."

"No," Sophia said, crying harder. "I ... I'm helping you. This is what's supposed to happen." She glanced to the broken tank beside them, shook her head, and said, "Not that."

He looked at the tank and then closed his eyes. His breathing became more laboured and there was a rattling in his chest that shook his entire body. Sophia reached for his thanatometer. His death age had already fallen four years and it continued to quickly tick down towards his age. Blood fell from the cut on Sophia's cheek and dripped onto her grandpa's forehead. She cleaned the blood from his face.

"How does the air taste?" she asked. "Real air? How does it feel in your lungs?"

He slowly opened his eyes. His expression had changed from anger to exhaustion.

Sophia smiled through tears. "Feels good doesn't it?" she said, glancing at his thanatometer again:

PDA 146.4

Age 146.2

Sophia stopped smiling. "I'm sorry it had to be this way," she said. "I'm sorry I wasn't a better granddaughter and that I didn't come sooner." She sniffed and wiped her eyes. "I don't wanna die either. But I can't hide from it anymore. And now, neither can you."

PDA 146.2

The old man looked up at Sophia and his wheezing stopped. Then his head flopped to the side and a final breath rattled out of his lungs.

Sophia closed her grandfather's lifeless eyes and slid out from under him, gently placing his head on the floor.

At that moment, Rubin burst through the bedroom door. Sophia jumped to her feet. Both of them stood still, Rubin examining the dead body of Dr. Léon Rousseau, Sophia examining Rubin.

"What did you do?" he asked.

"What I had to," she said, wiping her face with her palm.

Rubin stepped forward, almost slipping on the synthetic amniotic fluid coating the floor. He continued to the body cautiously and squatted down to look at the man's thanatometer. Rubin groaned when he realized the man was truly dead; he hadn't expected such violence from Sophia. He would've hurried inside if he had known what she was planning. He could have stopped her.

"You have to come with me," he said without looking up at her.

"Are you arresting me?"

"I'm not a cop."

"Then who are you?"

Rubin stood and faced Sophia, noticing for the first time that she was bleeding.

"You're hurt," he said, reaching out and taking hold of Sophia's face.

He turned Sophia's head to the side to examine the cut on her cheek and lifted her arm to inspect her other gash; she let him.

"Your lacerations need attention right away."

"Are you a doctor?"

"Yes."

"I hate doctors."

"Well, you need one right now, and I need to get you out of here."

Rubin grabbed her arm and tried to lead her out of the room, but Sophia pulled away from him.

"I'm not going anywhere."

"Do you want to be arrested? Is that why you did this?"

"No. I did it because it had to be done. And now I have to deal with the consequences."

"Really? You're ready to deal with jail for the rest of your life?"

Sophia shrugged and said, "Doesn't sound so bad."

"You really want to spend your last three months in jail?"

Sophia staggered backwards. "How do you know that?" she asked.

"Oh God, I just do okay," Rubin said, throwing his hands up in exasperation. "We've got to go."

"No," Sophia said, "not until you tell me how you know me?"

"If I promise to tell you everything in the car, will you come with me now?"

Sophia nodded hesitantly.

"Then let's go."

Rubin led Sophia out of the room. As they entered the hall, Sophia glanced back at her grandfather's body.

At the top of the stairs, Rubin heard someone running on the floor below. He pulled Sophia into a dark corner beside the old pew, shhed her, and held his breath.

The nurse ran up the stairs and down the hall towards the open bedroom door. Rubin grabbed Sophia's hand and together they snuck down the steps. When they were halfway down, they heard the nurse scream, which caused them to hurry down the rest of the stairs and run for the front door. They slipped outside, Sophia closing the door behind them, and raced to the car. Before driving off, Rubin glanced back at the house to see if the nurse had followed them outside; she hadn't, and the street was deserted.

"Home," Rubin yelled into the car's navigation system.

As they drove away, Sophia said, "Now you have to tell me who you are and how you know me."

"First, you tell why the hell you did that back there?"

"Did what?"

"Killed your grandfather!"

"I didn't kill him," Sophia said, looking out the window at the passing streetlights. "He'd been dead for years."

"He could have lived for at least five more years. You had no right to do that."

Sophia turned back to Rubin and said, "You call *that* living? Not eating or drinking or even breathing by yourself? That's not living, it's torture."

Rubin stared at Sophia, silently conceding. Her grandfather had been alive without actually living his life.

"If it was torture," Rubin said, "he was doing it to himself. It was his choice."

"It doesn't matter. He's better off now," Sophia said.

"Did you go there to do that?" Rubin asked.

"No. I just wanted to see him. And when I saw him floating there in the tank, I couldn't stop myself from … and then, you came."

"Right."

Rubin faced forward. Watching the road, he remembered that they were going to his house; he didn't know whether or not it was a good idea but he couldn't think of anywhere else to take her.

"Please tell me who you are," Sophia said.

"My name's Rubin Russell and I work for National Wellness."

"Of course you do," Sophia said, leaning back in her seat. "I should've known that."

"I met you the day you were born. I was assigned to monitor you."

"Why?"

"To develop an explanation for your PDA and to record what happens to you when you turn twenty-seven."

"And? What have you found?"

Rubin looked at Sophia. She seemed eager to hear what he had to say, almost hopeful that he had some answers for her.

"Nothing," Rubin said, shaking his head.

Sophia's expression went flat, and Rubin looked out the windshield again.

"There's no explanation."

"What do my doctors think will happen to me?"

"They think you'll somehow die of old age at twenty-seven."

"But you don't agree with them?"

"I don't know. I don't know what to believe."

For a moment, neither of them spoke. Rubin stared out the windshield. Sophia stared at him, slowly realizing who he was.

"It was you wasn't it?" Sophia asked, becoming more animated. "They stuck me with something and were about to throw me into the back of that cop car when you showed up and somehow convinced them to take me back to my apartment. Holy shit! I can't believe it. How did you do it? Why'd you do it?"

Rubin kept looking forward. He shook his head slightly and closed his eyes. "I told them you were my patient, and they released you into my care," he said, opening his eyes and looking at the road again.

"But why?"

"Same reason you're in my car now I guess."

"Which is?"

Rubin turned to her. She was young, strong, healthy. She had the vigor of youth that most people her age had except, with Sophia, it was a façade. Rubin glanced at her thanatometer and then back into her eyes. She was sickly and feeble and about to die. She was that fragile little baby again that needed to be held.

He watched the excitement fade from Sophia's face as he stared at her without responding to her question.

She seemed to regret asking, and he regretted not answering.

"Where can I take you until this thing blows over?" Rubin asked, checking his rearview mirror. "They're going to be looking everywhere for whoever did it. You'll have to hide for a while."

"I don't have time to hide."

"Well, you're going to have to make time," Rubin said. "Is there a safe place, other than your apartment, that you can go? Where nobody would think to look for you?"

Sophia faced forward and let her head fall back against the headrest. She watched the dark concrete streak beneath the car, escaping the accusatory glare of the headlights like a black lake of scurrying cockroaches. All at once, the energy drained out of her. She felt as if she couldn't even lift her arms; not to clean the dried blood off her face or to brush the hair out of her eyes. It was as though she'd finally stopped running the longest marathon of her life.

"Go to the corner of Orchard Street and First Ave," she said, closing her eyes. "Number 19."

"What's there?" Rubin asked.

Sophia turned onto her side away from Rubin. "A safe place," she said, sinking deeper into the seat and dozing off.

As Rubin spoke the new address into the car's navigation system, he thought he recognized it but couldn't remember why. He just hoped it was a place where nobody would think to look for Sophia, if anyone thought to look for her at all. He didn't know whether or not she'd be suspected in her grandfather's death, but if she was, he could give her an alibi. He was the only person with access to Sophia's locator so he could say she was anywhere else at the time of her grandfather's death. He hoped the authorities wouldn't come to him though because then he'd have to make up his own alibi as well. Helping Sophia get away could be seen as the same as murdering Dr. Rousseau in the eyes of some judges, and they would receive the maximum sentence. Even though Dr. Rousseau had only been alive on a computer screen, he had been the oldest living person in the world—punishment would be swift and unmerciful.

If caught, Rubin knew he could live through any prison term, but Sophia wouldn't, and Rubin wasn't going to let her die behind bars. He'd keep her out of jail until her birthday and then, if she lived past it, he'd place her under the custody of National Wellness.

Rubin looked at Sophia; curled up on the seat beside him, she slept. He wanted to reach out and place his hand on her back, to tell her that everything was going to be okay, to reassure her that he'd keep her safe. But he figured she probably already knew or didn't care, so he kept his hands on the steering wheel and faced forward again.

He glanced in the rearview mirror every few second, watching for the flashing lights of a police cruiser he imagined to be following them.

TWENTY-ONE

Sophia woke up to a bright streetlight shining into her face through the passenger side window of Rubin's car; it was still dark out, but the artificial light felt as bright as the sun. Recoiling from the glare, she turned away from the window and noticed that Rubin was gone. The keys were also missing from the ignition and the doors were locked. When Sophia sat up to look for him outside, she noticed that the cuts on her arm were bandaged, the dried blood gone. She raised her hand to her face and felt another bandage on her cheek. Her cuts didn't hurt anymore either. Sophia suddenly wanted to find Rubin even more and thank him for dressing her wounds. Thank him for keeping her out of jail, twice. She searched the dark streets and buildings outside the car. When she couldn't find him, she pushed a button on the console and the passenger door opened. Standing on the street beside the car, she still couldn't see Rubin anywhere, but she recognized Zurie's building across the street from her. The car door began to shut automatically. Sophia crossed the street.

She knocked softly; it was four in the morning, and she didn't want to wake the old woman. When nobody answered, she knocked a little louder. The door flew open.

"Come in. Come in," Zurie said, appearing wide awake and irritated by the interruption. "It's not time to open the door yet."

Zurie left the door open, marched down the hall, and disappeared into a room Sophia had never been in before. Sophia stepped inside and shut the door. She followed Zurie into a small, hazy room, lit only by candlelight, where incense burned, a woman lay on a single bed, Rubin sat in a chair at the foot of the bed, Zurie sat beside the woman, and a vacant chair faced Zurie on the other side of the bed.

"Take your seat, child," Zurie said, gesturing to the empty chair.

Rubin sat perfectly still. Sophia thought it strange that he hadn't turned around to look at her. She wondered if he was okay.

"Sit," Zurie said more forcefully.

Sophia sat down across from her and looked at the woman lying in the bed. Even in the low light Sophia could see how pale the elderly woman's face was as she lay stretched out on the bed, her mouth open, the left side of her bottom lip drooping down as if it were made of wax and melting—she looked dead.

"What's wrong with her?" Sophia asked.

"This is Ellie," Zurie said. "She's dying."

"Do you condone this?" Rubin asked, turning to Sophia.

Zurie glared at Rubin and said, "You promised not to speak after she entered."

"I know," Rubin said, turning to Zurie, "but there are places for people in her condition. Homes where people withdraw," Rubin said.

"People come here to die. They go to your *homes* to withdraw," Zurie said.

Rubin faced Sophia again and said, "Is this what you come here for? To watch people die?"

"No. I've never done this before."

"Then don't start now. I can take you to my house. You'll be safe there."

"Here's where she belongs," Zurie said. "Now be quiet and let her help."

Rubin stood up. "Come on, Sophia, let's go," he said. "You have enough to worry about without this."

Sophia looked from Zurie to Rubin and said, "But I don't even know who you are."

"I told you already."

"Right, you work for National Wellness and you've been watching me. How do I know you're not just going to take me to the cops or lock me up in a hospital room?"

"I brought you here didn't I," Rubin said.

"Enough," Zurie said. "Leave it. Respect the death bed."

"Come on," Rubin said, gesturing towards the door.

Sophia glanced at the door and then at the dying woman. "This is a safe place. Trust me," she said to Rubin before turning to Zurie. "What do I have to do?"

Zurie stared at Sophia and nodded. "Take her hand, child," she said, taking hold of Ellie's right hand.

Sophia took Ellie's clammy hand in hers, and Rubin reluctantly sat back down at the foot of the bed.

"What now?" Sophia asked.

"We wait."

After a few minutes, Ellie opened her eyes and looked at Sophia. "Kitty," she said, her voice weak, her lungs wheezing with each breath. "What are you doing here?"

"I'm not," Sophia said before stopping herself and looking at Zurie.

"She came to be with you," Zurie said. "She came to take you home."

"Oh Kitty," Ellie said, squeezing Sophia's hand, a faint smile on her face. She shut her eyes. "Thank you for coming. I missed you."

Sophia smiled back and said, "You don't have to thank me."

Ellie lost consciousness before responding.

"It won't be long now," Zurie said. "They always wait for someone. Today, it's you."

A few hours later, Rubin sleeping in his chair, Ellie's last breath rattled out of her chest while Sophia and Zurie held her limp hands tightly. Zurie bowed her head, and Sophia did the same.

When Zurie raised her head again, she said, "Now I can open the door."

She stood, left the room, and opened the front door. Sophia, still holding Ellie's lifeless hand, saw sunlight enter the hall and bedroom. A gust of fresh air blew into the room, and Sophia closed her eyes as the air caressed her face. She thought she could fall asleep sitting upright like Rubin.

"You can let go now, child," Zurie said, stepping back into the room.

Sophia opened her eyes and, without letting go, looked at Ellie's hand in hers.

Zurie grabbed a white sheet and placed it on the edge of the bed. "You helped her go home," she said, standing still beside the bed.

"I didn't do anything," Sophia said. "I just sat here."

"You did everything," Zurie said, stepping towards Sophia and placing a hand on her shoulder. "Let go now, child. She can't leave if you're holding on. Let go."

Sophia slid her hand out from underneath Ellie's and watched Zurie cover the body with the sheet. Then she stood and, realizing that she ached all over and was extremely thirsty, left the bedroom. Walking past Rubin still asleep in his chair, she made her way into the kitchen, turned on the tap and stuck her mouth under the faucet. She drank until her stomach was full. When she turned off the water and stood up straight again, the glowing display of her thanatometer drew her eyes. She looked down at the twenty-seven and her stomach turned. Suddenly nauseated, she hunched over the sink and vomited.

"It's okay, child," Zurie said, entering the kitchen and placing a hand on Sophia's back.

Sophia spit, washed her vomit down the sink, and rinsed her mouth.

"Sorry," she said, taking another sip of water before turning to face the old woman.

"Don't be. Death is disgusting at first. But now you've seen both kinds, messy and clean."

"Why am I sick?" Sophia asked, wiping her mouth.

"Hard to say. Fear. Poison."

"What do you mean poison?"

"That thing on your wrist makes you sick. Show people what it says and then get rid of it."

Sophia took a deep breath, her nausea subsiding.

Zurie patted Sophia's shoulder and said, "First drink, then rest. Go sit."

Sophia sat down at the table and watched the old woman make tea. As the water heated, Zurie placed a teacup and a plate of crackers and hummus on the table. Sophia ate slowly, afraid of unsettling her stomach, but the more she ate the better she felt. By the time the tea was ready, she had eaten half the plate of food.

Sophia took a sip of tea. "Do you really think my thanatometer is making me sick?" she asked.

"Sure," Zurie said. She took a sip of tea. "Either it's poisoning you or you think it's poisoning you. Either way, you're sick."

Sophia watched the steam rise from her cup and said, "Do you think I'll die in three months?"

Zurie put her cup down and stared at Sophia for a long time before responding. "Hard to say," she said. "Maybe, maybe not. But you must be ready for both." She took a sip. "And neither. Just like everyone."

Sophia finished her tea and then leaned forward, stretched her left arm across the table, and rested her head on her arm.

"I killed my grandfather," she said, closing her eyes. "He was floating in a tank and being kept alive by computers. He couldn't even open his eyes without my help."

"What happened?"

"I broke the tank, and he died in my arms."

"You didn't kill him, child. You set him free."

"Is that why I don't feel bad about it? 'Cause I don't. I'm glad I did it. And I think, right before the end, he was glad too."

"Shh, child. There has been too much talk of death this day," Zurie said, placing her hand on Sophia's head. "Sleep now and dream of life."

Then Zurie, keeping her hand on the side of Sophia's head, began to hum a deep and somber song of only four notes. It comforted Sophia even though she didn't recognize the melody. The song somehow articulated exactly how she felt at that moment; it expressed what her heart knew and her mouth couldn't say.

Listening to Zurie's song, Sophia fell into a deep, dreamless sleep.

TWENTY-TWO

On the morning of Sophia's twenty-sixth birthday, her mother picked her up in front of her apartment.

"Where are we going?" Sophia asked, from the passenger seat.

"It's a surprise," Lizette said, glancing at Sophia and smirking.

"What are you up to?"

"You'll see. We're almost there."

When they finally stopped in front of the Skylark Haven Rest Home, Sophia stared out the passenger window at the sky blue four-story complex and her mouth fell open.

"Ah, Mum?"

"Yeah?"

"What are we doing here?"

Lizette leaned over to see what Sophia was looking at. "Do you like it?" she asked, excitedly patting her daughter's leg.

"That depends," Sophia said, still looking out her window.

Lizette sat back in her seat. "On what?" she asked.

"On why we're here," Sophia said, turning to her mum and looking unimpressed.

For a second, Lizette's excitement faltered, but she quickly opened both car doors and said, "Come on. Let's go look."

Reluctantly, Sophia exited the car. She stood up, crossed her arms, and surveyed the grounds; perfectly manicured grass, trees, hedges, rose brushes surrounded the facility and a concrete ramp led to the entrance. It was a way station for the old and dying, the thriving vegetation enveloping the outside of the building an insult to the decay happening inside. Sophia expected the bodies of the recently deceased, on gurneys and zipped up in black rubber bags, to be wheeled out of the building and down the ramp towards her at any minute.

"What do you think?" Lizette said, stepping beside Sophia and looking at the building with her hands on her hips. "Do you like it?"

Sophia turned to her mum and said, "Why are we here?" in an accusatory tone.

"Because your father and I," Lizette began, still looking at the building, "have reserved a room here for when it's our time to withdraw."

"Yeah but, don't you have like another seventy years before you have to start worrying about that?"

"Yes, well," Lizette said, glancing at Sophia, "you have to book early."

"Why'd you bring me here?" Sophia asked, trying not to sound as resentful as she felt for being taken to a nursing home on her birthday.

Lizette looked at Sophia, her smile faltering, and said, "I wanted you to see it before …"

Lizette's happy expression suddenly contorted with grief. She hunched forward and buried her face into her hands; she was completely silent for a moment, not even breathing, her shoulders jerking up and down as she tried to hold back tears.

"Mum, please don't cry," Sophia said, putting a hand on her mother's back, begrudging the comfort she felt force to give.

Lizette lowered her hands, inhaled loudly, and stood up straight again, "I'm sorry," she said. "I just … I'm fine."

Sophia dropped her hand back to her side. "Are you sure?" she asked, only partially caring.

She wiped her eyes and feigned a smile. "Yeah, I'm fine," she said, moving forward. "Let's go inside."

Sophia didn't move. "No," she said, shaking her head. "I don't think I want to."

Lizette turned back and stepped in front of Sophia. "Why not?"

She looked into her mother's eyes—she seemed hurt and confused, but Sophia didn't believe her confusion.

"I brought you here so you could see it," Lizette said. "Where we'd be when it's our time. So that you'd know we'd be taken care of."

"You're such a liar," Sophia scoffed. "Why don't you just say it?"

"Say what?"

"I'm not an idiot, mum. And when you bring me to a place like this a year before ..." Sophia stopped herself. She turned away from Lizette and shook her head. "Let's just go. Take me home, please."

Sophia opened the passenger side door, and Lizette stepped in front of her.

"We're not going anywhere until you tell me what you're so angry about," Lizette said, tears still in her eyes. "I brought you here because I thought it would be fun but if I would've known that you'd react like this I'd have—"

"You brought me here to admit me," Sophia yelled. "And you can't own up to it."

Lizette drew back and said, "I, I didn't bring you here to—"

"Yes, you did. Just admit it. You've got seventy more years before you have to worry about going to a place like this. Probably more."

Sophia grabbed Lizette's wrist and looked at her thanatometer. Lizette pulled her arm away.

"Seventy-two years. Even better. And I've got one. So tell me," Sophia said, pointing at the nursing home. "Who's this place for?"

Without speaking, Lizette lowered her head and looked at the ground.

"That's what I thought." She got into the car and said, "Take me home," before shutting the door.

On the drive back, neither of them spoke. When they stopped in front of Sophia's building, Sophia reached for the button to open her door; Lizette put her hand over the button and locked the doors.

"What are you doing?" Sophia asked. "Let me out please."

"That place wasn't for you."

"Really?" Sophia said, leaning back against the door and crossing her arms.

"It's for your father and me but we booked it early because we want you to start thinking about what you would like to do when your time is closer. We thought we could all arrange our withdrawing places together. At the same time."

"And where would you like me to go then? Because I'm sure you and dad have a place all picked out."

Lizette took her hand from the console and pulled her tablet from the bag in the back seat. She held it in the centre of the car so they could both see the screen.

"Your doctors actually recommended it to us."

"I'm sure they did."

When Lizette touched the screen, images of a hospital room—trying desperately to look like an apartment but failing miserably—appeared. It had its own big bathroom, a large window with a view of downtown in one corner, a plaid couch beneath it, a desk in the other corner, light oak flooring, blue and white walls, and a hospital bed in the centre of the room equipped with thanatometer armrest, metal guardrails, and diagnostic computer. The bed was a prison; Sophia wanted to break the tablet over her knee and toss it out the window. She stared at the button to open her door; she wanted to push it and run down the street.

"They said there's a pool and a gym and meditation cabins in the forest behind the hospital," Lizette said, scrolling down through images. "There's also gardens and a lake and—"

"I don't care," Sophia said.

Lizette shrank back into her seat with her tablet in her lap. "You have to start thinking about this, Sophia," she said. "You need to prepare."

"How? By sitting in a room and waiting to die? No thanks."

Sophia opened her door and stepped out of the car. She didn't know why she kept seeing her mum. She always felt worse afterwards. She never parted ways with her and thought, *That was fun. Why don't we do that more often.* As she was walking away, she heard a car door open but didn't turn around.

"Sophie," Lizette called. "Please come back."

Sophia shook her head while continuing to walk away. Lizette ran after her.

When she caught up to Sophia, she stood in front of her and said, "Why won't you talk to me?"

"There's nothing to say," Sophia said without looking at her mother and continuing to walk away. "Leave me alone."

Lizette stopped walking. "Please stop," she said, standing still.

Sophia kept up her pace without wavering.

"You had a brother," Lizette yelled.

Sophia halted. She spun around and looked incredulously at her mother.

"God, I'm sorry," Lizette said, dropping her head and rubbing her eyes. "That's not the way I wanted to …"

"How? When?"

"Get back into the car and I'll tell you."

"No," Sophia said, moving towards her mum. "Tell me now."

Lizette glanced around to see if anyone was around. When she saw that they were alone, she said, "You were eight. The doctors still couldn't explain your PDA."

"What does this have to do with my brother?"

"Let's go sit in the car," Lizette said, gesturing back to where she'd parked.

"Why didn't you tell me about him sooner?"

"Because I didn't know how to tell you. But I always thought you should know."

"Well."

"Well, like I said, you were eight and—"

"And what? Just tell me what happened to him."

"Your father doesn't even know, okay," Lizette snapped. "And I haven't spoken about this to anyone in eighteen years. This isn't easy for me."

"Did you have an affair?" Sophia asked, her voice flat.

"No. Of course not. He was your father's son."

"Then why doesn't he know?"

"Because I had an abortion."

"What? Why?"

"Our procreation permit was revoked. They were afraid another child would …"

"Would what? Be like me?" Sophia asked.

Lizette nodded.

"So they made you abort?"

"No, but they would have if I refused."

"Oh my God," Sophia said, spinning around and looking up at the cloudy sky. When she faced her mum again, she said, "And dad doesn't know?"

Lizette shook her head.

"Why'd you tell me?"

Lizette stared blankly at her daughter. Beneath the rage she saw in Sophia's face her own anguish reflected back at her; at first she felt guilty for sharing her pain with Sophia but the guilt was diminished by a feeling of immense relief, almost euphoria. At that moment she realized her motivation for telling Sophia—she couldn't bear the burden alone anymore and Sophia was the only other person who would fully understand and absorb the grief as her own.

"You're unbelievable," Sophia said, marching away from her mum and then back towards her again. "Would you have done the same to me if you'd known about my death age before I was born?"

As Sophia looked into her mother's eyes waiting for her to become enraged at the accusation and cry out, *No, of course not, how dare you*, her mother's stillness and stunned expression confessed the truth.

Sophia turned, and ran away, her pace quickening each time Lizette called out to her. At first, Sophia wished she had been aborted, she hadn't asked to be alive and destined to die young. Had her mother done it, her regret would have punished her every day of her life, the way living with the abortion of her brother must have for eighteen years, and she would've deserved it.

Sophia sprinted until she could no longer hear her mother's cries, and then she thought of her mother, alone in a room with a doctor, aborting her child. Sophia couldn't believe what her mother had gone through alone, the worst decision to have to make and the worst choice to have to live with done without support from anyone. Sophia was glad that she was there to hear what no one else had, to be there for her mother. She stopped running, her lungs gasping for breath, sweat beginning to tickle her pores. She felt suddenly grateful to be alive, knowing that her brother would have been grateful too had their mother chosen life and later had told him how close he'd come to oblivion.

Sophia turned back and thought about running to her mother and hugging her, but she quickly pushed the thought out of her mind and continued to walk away. She couldn't forgive her. She wouldn't let herself. She also wouldn't let herself forget her brother—he was the only person who would have truly understood and loved her. The only person with whom she could have shared a common fate. But he didn't exist because of Lizette, because of the doctors, because anyone who won't live over a century doesn't deserve to live at all.

Sophia closed her eyes and imagined her brother being the same age as her. He was her twin only taller, with shorter hair, and their father's square jaw. When he waved at her, Sophia saw that he wasn't wearing a thanatometer. He didn't know when he was going to die, and Sophia envied him for it.

Dr. Léon Rousseau Killed at 146, Six Years Before His PDA

Dr. Léon Gabriel Rousseau, the world's oldest living person for the past eight years, died early this morning after an unknown assailant threw a computer screen, monitoring the doctor's own vital signs, into one of the glass panes of his longevity chamber. The chamber shattered and forced Dr. Rousseau into the open air, disconnecting him from his life support systems. He died on the floor of his bedroom. He was 146.

When the on-duty nurse heard the glass break, she rushed to his aid. Finding him alone, she promptly administered CPR. Unable to resuscitate him, the nurse phoned Dr. Andre Banks, Dr. Rousseau's longtime physician, who arrived moments later. Dr. Banks immediately contacted the authorities after examining the body and seeing the state of the room.

"It was apparent to me, that the chamber had been intentionally broken," said Dr. Banks before leaving the Rousseau home to conduct an autopsy of his patient.

When asked about the cause of death, Dr. Banks said, "He most likely died of a heart attack. The sudden shock of being out of the chamber would have put a lot of stress on his body and probably sent him into cardiac arrest. However, I'll know more after I've completed the autopsy."

When asked how long Dr. Rousseau would have lived had the chamber not been broken, Dr. Banks said, "Six years at the very least. His PDA increased steadily and all his vital signs were in the green."

An autopsy is currently underway.

An intensive police investigation is also underway.

"It appears that someone gained entry into the house with the intension of breaking the victim's chamber and killing him," said Detective Robert Aiken, an officer with the Robbery Homicide division. "There is no sign of forced entry and nothing appears to have been stolen."

Asked if members of the group Death by Natural Causes, DNC, are suspected of perpetrating the crime against Dr. Rousseau, Detective Aiken said, "We aren't ruling anything out. All suspects will be interviewed and all avenues will be explored in order to bring the perpetrators to justice."

The DNC have been extremely vocal in their opposition to what they consider to be "the methods of unnaturally sustaining life"—longevity chambers being the primary objection of the group. The DNC has called for the "natural death" of Dr. Rousseau several times over the past few years, claiming that the suffering he endures inside the chamber is inhumane and sadistic. Various group members are wanted in connection with numerous murders around the world, "mercy killings" to the DNC. They have been known to disconnect every different kind of life sustaining apparatus in order to give their victims "a natural death."

"It's murder," said Detective Aiken. "And just because they call their unnatural acts natural doesn't make it so."

So far the DNC has not claimed responsibility for the slaying of Dr. Rousseau, but the police say they expect to have the culprits in custody within the next few days.

As the police continue with their investigation, the world begins to grieve the loss of its eldest person. Upon verification of his claim to be the world's oldest person ten years ago, Dr. Léon Gabriel Rousseau's house became a popular pilgrimage site. For two years, as is customary for the succeeding eldest, his doors were open to anyone who wanted to meet him. In that time he saw thousands of people and inspired millions more around the world.

Tonight at 5:02pm—the exact time of Dr. Léon Rousseau's birth—five minutes of silence will be observed around the world. Memorial service to be announced within the next few days.

The oldest person in the world is now Katsu Godo, 140, who lives in Japan, said Tabitha Spencer, CEO of National Wellness. Preparations are currently underway in Japan for the induction ceremony to follow Dr. Rousseau's memorial service.

Sitting inside Rubin's car beside the Skylark Haven sign, Sophia read the article about her grandfather off Rubin's tablet screen. She felt relieved not to be mentioned as a suspect but like a coward to be hiding from what she had done, what she thought was right.

Sophia hadn't heard of the DNC before and, even though they sounded like terrorists, thought about finding their leader and joining them, but the feeling quickly passed; she hadn't gone to her grandpa's house to give him a natural death and she didn't want to go around mercy killing everyone on life support systems.

I'm not a murderer. Am I?

Her grandpa had wanted it right before the end. Would have asked for it if he could have. If anyone would have listened.

I'm the only one who had. Aren't I?

She couldn't disagree with what the DNC was doing, but she also couldn't join them. Even if there were countless others like her grandpa, she never wanted to be responsible for another person's death ever again.

Rubin watched Sophia's eyes move back and forth across the screen. His first instinct after reading the article at Zurie's house was to hide it from Sophia so that she didn't have to think about it more than she probably already was, but he decided on the drive to the nursing home that she had to read it. Even if it scared her or made her feel guilty, she had to read it.

Sophia looked up from the tablet and turned to Rubin, the expression of concern on her face making Rubin second-guess himself.

"How many people use life support to stay alive longer?" she asked.

"Hundreds of thousands," Rubin said. "Maybe millions. Everyone uses something when they're close to the end."

Sophia gazed at Rubin. She appeared to be on the verge of tears.

"Are you okay?" Rubin asked.

"I don't know," she said, looking back down at the article. "I thought it was the right thing to do but wouldn't that make it right for the millions of people out there who just aren't ready to die?"

Rubin took the tablet from Sophia and said, "You were right when you said that he wasn't really living, but he was alive. Just like all the other people using something to prolong their lives. Maybe your grandpa's better off now. Maybe everyone on life support would be better off dying. But all of them, including your grandpa, choose life over death just like anyone would."

"But it's not really a choice is it?" Sophia said. "Not when everyone would think you're crazy to say, 'No thanks doc, I think I'm gonna die next year instead of living for five more.' Where do you draw the line, huh? When people are just heads floating in jars for eternity?"

"And how do you decide when people should die?"

"They should die when they're supposed to," Sophia said, tugging at her thanatometer and grimacing.

Rubin reached over and put a hand over Sophia's. When she stopped pulling at her thanatometer and looked at him, he took his hand from hers.

"I should go," she said, glancing out the windshield at the sky blue building up ahead of them.

Rubin followed Sophia's eyes to the building and said, "Why are we here?"

"It's just something I need to do."

"I'll wait here," Rubin said, opening the passenger door.

Sophia smiled and exited the car. At the front door of the nursing home, Sophia glanced back at Rubin before entered the building. Inside, directly in front of Sophia, sat a nurse wearing a pink uniform. She sat completely still behind a desk, staring at Sophia. As she stepped forward and noticed the dull smile and rapidly blinking eyes, Sophia realized that the nurse was a robot.

"Hello. My name is Bridgette," the robot said in a chipper voice, its mouth moving slightly out of sink with its words. It had a bubblegum demeanor that matched its pink uniform. "Welcome to Skylark Haven. How may I help you?"

Sophia stepped up to the desk and examined the robot. Its name tag spelled Bridgette in gold letters. Its wig didn't have a single hair out of place, and its skin, although appearing real, stretched in odd, unnatural ways around its mouth. As Sophia studied the robot, it tilted its head and moved a hand past its ear, as if to tuck hair back behind its ear, but its hair was already tucked back.

"Hi," Sophia said, looking around for a real person.

"Hello. Are you here to visit someone? May I help direct you to his or her room?"

"I'd like a tour please."

"Certainly. If you will just sign in," Bridgette said, gesturing to the computer screen and stylus on the desk, "then we can take you on a tour of the facilities."

Sophia took up the stylus and signed the name Stephanie Cunningham onto the tablet, the name of a girl in her elementary school who used to call her Ms. Dies Tomorrow because of the tape on her thanatometer. Sophia looked down at the name and thought about the last day of grade six when she pulled a fist-full of hair out of Stephanie's head, the shriek of pain that made her run home with a smile and bury the hair in her backyard. She wondered if Stephanie's hair was still there and regretted pulling it.

"Thank you, Stephanie," Bridgette said, still smiling that fake smile. "Here at Skylark Haven we strive to be the best withdrawing home in the world."

As Bridgette spoke, Sophia heard the low murmur of countless indiscernible voices and the clinking of glassware from behind a door to her left. She stepped towards it.

"Where are you going?" Bridgette asked.

"To look around," Sophia called back over her shoulder.

"Very well. Please sign out when you leave," Bridgette said before turning back to the front door.

Sophia stepped into the dining hall where a sea of silver hair and wrinkled faces bobbed up and down. There were a few younger people peppered into the mix, family members visiting for breakfast Sophia assumed. Nurses were there too, in pink uniforms, scurrying around filling water glasses and carting away dirty plates.

The hall looked like a restaurant she and her parents would have gone to. Natural light flooded in through the large windows around the room. The tiles beneath her feet were the colour of sand. The coffee-colored tables had green placemats on them that matched the bamboo plants scattered throughout the room. Her mum would love the bamboo, her dad the solid tables. She could picture her parents eating a delicious meal, one of their last, surrounded by friends to make them laugh and nurses to care for them.

Looking for an empty seat, Sophia saw many thanatometers with glowing cables running to small computers strapped around waists. Sophia stepped past a time-ravaged woman clinging to a walker with a clear tube running under her nose and down to an oxygen tank attached to the walker. Sophia smiled, but the woman either ignored her or was too preoccupied with her efforts to smile back.

Near the back of the dinning hall was a table of five with an empty chair. Sophia made her way to the table and stood behind the unoccupied chair, placing her hands on it. The conversation paused and nobody took another bite of oatmeal.

"Hello," Sophia said. "Is it alright if I join you?"
"Of course."

"Please do."

"Pull up a chair."

"Have a seat, dear."

One man said nothing; he simply ate his oatmeal and read from a tablet propped up in his hand.

Sophia smiled and sat down. Every person at the table was probably a century older than her.

"I'm Dorothy," said the curly grey-haired woman beside Sophia, placing her hand on her chest, a glowing cable attached to her thanatometer disappearing down beneath her chair.

"Nice to meet you, Dorothy."

Dorothy then pointed around the table and introduced each person in turn. "And this is Nikoli," she began, "Ravi, Jennifer, and that's Douglas over there reading rudely at the dining table."

Douglas grunted without looking up.

Douglas was the only person without a cable attached to his thanatometer.

"Don't mind him," Dorothy said, flicking her hand.

They all had short, grey hair. Ravi had black hairs mixed in with the grey on his head and the grey stubble on his face while Douglas and Nikoli were pure white and clean shaven. The three men wore collared shirts. The women blouses. Jennifer looked like a slighter version of Dorothy only with straight hair that framed her face.

"So, what brings you here?" Jennifer asked.

"My parents are going to withdraw here," Sophia said. "I just wanted to come see it before they do."

"Oh that's wonderf—"

"You mean die," Douglas said, looking up from his tablet, his voice gruff.

"Douglas," Dorothy hissed. "Really."

He spooned oatmeal into his mouth and swallowed. "There's no point sprinkling sugar on it to make it sweeter," Douglas said. "It's just the way it is." He then pointed with his oatmealy spoon as he spoke. "Ravi here hits his death age in six months. Nikoli in nine."

"That's enough Douglas," Ravi said, his melodic voice thick with an Indian accent.

Nikoli shifted in his seat.

"Death ages can change though," Jennifer said. "Just look at Dr. Léon Rousseau. He increased his more than anyone."

"Yeah but he's dead now too," Douglas said.

"Killed by those radicals," Dorothy said.

Jennifer nodded and said, "Yes, he could have lived a lot longer too."

"The man had lived long enough," Douglas scoffed. "Hell, he'd been living beyond his death age for years."

"He had almost six years before his time," Jennifer said, trying to scold Douglas. "And I heard that his death age increased by almost twenty years throughout his life. The most yet."

"I thought he'd live forever," Nikoli said. "I thought he'd figured out how."

"Do you remember when the last oldest died?" Dorothy asked.

"Uh huh."

"Nadira Nuti."

"That's right. One hundred and forty-two years old when she withdrew. Born with that age too."

"That's right. Born with it," Douglas said. "She didn't steal years by plugging into computers and living in an incubator for the last five years of her life."

"Well, it's terrible that the doctor's gone."

"It's a tragedy no matter what *anybody* says."

"Who's the oldest now? Anybody hear?"

"Katsu Godo, from Japan," Douglas said. "One hundred and forty."

"Six years younger than the doctor, but respectable."

"I visited him when his doors were open a few years ago," Ravi said. "Nice man, the doctor."

"Did you ever visit Dr. Rousseau, Sophia?" Dorothy asked.

"He was my grandfather," Sophia said.

Everyone at the table stared at Sophia without moving for a moment. Even Douglas took his eyes from his tablet.

"Sorry for your loss," Jennifer said.

The others nodded.

"Yes," Dorothy said. "We're all sorry. It is a terrible tragedy."

"It's not a tragedy," Sophia said, her face flushed.

"Excuse me dear?"

"My grandfather's death. It's not a tragedy. He lived, if you can even call it that, encased in glass, soaking in synthetic amniotic fluid with an oxygen mask around his face. He couldn't even open his eyes or speak or breathe on his own. It was his time."

"Ha!" Douglas cried as he smacked the table and made the cutlery bounce and everybody jump. He stared at Sophia with wide eyes. "Finally someone else in this place actually knows what they're talking about. You're right. You're absolutely right."

Glad to have someone on her side, Sophia grinned.

"I can't believe my ears," Dorothy said. "Your grandfather could have lived to be over one hundred and fifty years old. Maybe even one sixty. And you're happy he's dead?"

"I'm happy he can finally rest," Sophia said. "His body wanted to die years ago, but they got computers to do the work his organs couldn't anymore and kept him alive in a glass jar. If he didn't know when he was going to die, he would have just let it happen. Instead he was obsessed." She held up her thanatometer and said, "With this."

"Well," Jennifer began, puckering her lips and scowling at Sophia, "that's easy to say when you're one hundred years from your age, dear."

Sophia turned to Jennifer and held out her thanatometer to her. "Less than three months actually," she said, her heart pounding. "Even less than Ravi."

It felt good to just say it. And why not. It was the truth. She glanced at the confused expressions staring back at her and continued to hold out her arm.

Jennifer and Dorothy leaned over and looked down at the thanatometer. Dorothy covered her mouth and turned to the others.

"Is it?" Jennifer asked. "I can't see it."

Dorothy nodded.

"But, but you're just a kid," Ravi said. "It can't be true."

Sophia turned to Ravi and extended her arm towards him. "See for yourself," she said.

Ravi looked around at the others at the table. "I don't ... I mean it's not ..."

"Go on," Douglas said.

The little Indian man took hold of Sophia's wrist and glanced down. He then turned away and glanced down again, leaned in, and squinted, his mouth hanging open. Nikoli bent towards Sophia's thanatometer and stared with his forehead furrowed.

"Let me see," Douglas said, waving for her to come to him.

Sophia stood up and leaned across the table with her arm held out to him. Douglas took hold of her hand, examined, and grunted before looking up at Sophia and letting go of her hand. Sophia sat back down. She noticed that people at other tables were rubbernecking in her direction.

"How," Ravi finally asked, shaking his head.

"I have no idea," Sophia said. "That's just what it says."

"Has it always?" Dorothy asked.

"Yes."

"Are you sick?" asked Nikoli.

"No."

"Is it …" Jennifer leaned forward and whispered, "Is it right?"

"Of course it's right," Ravi declared.

Douglas threw his spoon down into his bowl and eyed Ravi. "Why of course? Why always of course?"

"Oh, Douglas, not now."

"Why can't it be wrong?" Douglas said, slapping the table again and pointing at Sophia. "She's a kid. Twenty-six. Healthy. Are we supposed to believe that piece of junk on her arm? Huh?" He paused and then looked at Sophia. "Tell them."

"Tell them what?"

"Tell them what you think of that thing."

She looked at her thanatometer. "I hate it," she said. "It's run my life for so long it's hard not to hate it. The happiest times in my life were during fittings. That moment between the old thana being removed and the new one being put on. If I imagine not having one, I get a taste of that happiness."

Ravi stared at Sophia. "How do you imagine not having a thanatometer?" he asked.

"Can you remember that feeling? Of being fifteen, or ten, or even five and without a thana for a few seconds?"

"Of course," Douglas said.

"I think so."

"Maybe."

"I don't know."

"I don't know either."

"It's like meditating. Just relax and picture it."

Other than Douglas, they all looked at her as if she were crazy.

"Close your eyes," Sophia said, leaning back in her chair.

Nobody shut their eyes.

"Just for a minute."

Slowly, all five of them exchanged looks and then shut their eyes. Dorothy and Jennifer shifted in their seats.

"Now picture that moment," Sophia said. "That moment when the thanatometer left your wrist. And when you've found it, hold onto it and let the feeling fill you up."

Sophia closed her eyes too and indulged in the feeling. Weightlessness took hold of her. She felt as if she were light enough to float up out of her chair. Then she opened her eyes and felt the heavy weight of her body again.

Everyone sat up slightly. Ravi swayed.

"Feel that weight lifting. Feel the calm moving through your entire body."

Sophia glanced around at the five of them, beaming, her eyes wrinkling in the corners, her cheeks starting to hurt from smiling; they looked peaceful. She felt useful. As if she were doing something important. Something that mattered. She let her smile fade and told them to open their eyes.

When all eyes where on her, she told them to look at their thanatometers and feel the tremendous weight of them. As they looked down, a visible heaviness slumped their bodies forward.

"Oh my," Ravi cried out. "My PDA. It, it went up."

"Really?" Sophia asked, leaning forward.

"What?" said Dorothy

"How much?" asked Douglas.

"Three months," Ravi said, grinning and looking around at the others. "It went up three months.

"Mine too," said Dorothy.

"I can't believe," Nikoli said, staring down at his thanatometer. "Mine went up two months."

"That's how much mine went up too," said Jennifer.

"Douglas," said Ravi. "How about yours?"

"Five months," he said, dazed.

Dorothy turned to the table beside them and said, "My PDA went up three months." She extended her thanatometer out to the people sitting at the table. "From meditating."

The entire dining room buzzed with conversation, and all the residents began to slowly gravitate towards Sophia's table.

What the hell just happened? Sophia thought, looking at the five elderly people in front of her.

She started to stand when Douglas's face twisted into a grimace; he looked as if his meal had gone sour in his stomach. "Wait," he yelled, holding up his non-thanatometer arm while staring down. "Four mon … no, three … two."

"Mines back where it started," Nikoli cried.

"Mine too," said Dorothy

All five of them looked shriveled and old again. Even more so than before.

Sophia glanced at her thanatometer—the numbers hadn't moved, but she knew they hadn't even before looking. She stood, slipped past the gathering crowd, and left the dining hall. She rushed past the reception desk towards the front entrance.

"Hello, Stephanie," Bridgette, said, eyeing Sophia. "Please sign out before you leave."

Sophia hurried outside without signing. She stood still for a moment in the hot morning sun, squinting at the glare coming off Rubin's car, before making her way towards it.

"Wait," Douglas called from the entrance.

Sophia spun around. Holding his tablet in one hand, he panted, sweat beading on his face, and had to lean up against the door to steady himself. Douglas seemed ancient and exhausted, not as strong as he had sitting at the table.

"Wait," he said again, continuing to Sophia with his tablet held out. "This is you isn't it?"

Sophia took the tablet and looked down. The article on the screen was titled *Death at 27*, and it was dated the day after she was born. She read the article quickly. There it was for all to see. Her secret that, until recently, she had kept from everyone—twenty-seven.

"Where did you get this?"

Still out of breath Douglas said, "I saved it. I save all the ones they don't want us to remember."

"Thank you," she said. "I needed to see this."

Douglas took back his tablet. He squinted at the screen and scrolled furiously. When he had apparently found what he was looking for, he faced Sophia and passed the tablet back to her. "Did you do it?" he said, his face hardened.

Sophia looked down at the article about her grandfather that she had read in Rubin's car and then looked back into Douglas's eyes.

"Did you?"

"Yeah. I helped him die."

Douglas nodded without speaking. Sophia turned and walked away, but turned back after a few steps, ran up to Douglas, and threw her arms around the old man's neck.

"Thanks," she said, squeezing tightly.

Douglas hugged her back and said, "You did the right thing."

Sophia let go, smiled, and began walking towards Rubin, who was now standing beside the car with the driver-side door open.

When Sophia was halfway to the car, Douglas held up his thanatometer and yelled, "I'll get rid of this thing as soon as I get the chance."

She turned and smiled. "Me too," she yelled back.

"Everything go okay?" Rubin asked when Sophia was standing across the car from him.

She nodded, a broad smile lighting up her face.

Rubin couldn't remember ever seeing her look as happy as she appeared at that moment. "What happened in there?" he asked.

"I'll tell you in the car."

As they drove away, Sophia stared at Douglas through the passenger side mirror. He stood where she'd left him with his hand held up in a wave. She waved back and watched him shrink away into the distance.

TWENTY-FOUR

Sophia and Zack sat meditating on the wood floor of his quiet apartment. They faced each other, legs crossed, eyes closed, hands relaxed in their laps with fingers resting on top of each other and tips of thumbs touching. The sun shone through the living room window, stretching across the floor and bathing both of them in warm light.

Sophia imagined herself on a stage in the park, meditating in front of thousands of people who followed her lead. Then she inhaled deeply and thought of nothing but the darkness behind her eyelids. At the bottom of her exhale, in the natural pause between breaths, she was back on the stage. She was about to turn twenty-seven. All the people in front of her opened their eyes; everyone could see her age, 26.99, and waited to see what would happen to her. Sophia inhaled again into darkness and thoughtlessness. Exhaling back onto the stage where it was midnight, the first minute of her twenty-seventh year. Time stopped. She stood and walked through the motionless crowd. As Sophia strolled among the crowd, everyone continued to look up at the stage to where she had been. She turned, looked back to see what everyone was looking at, and saw herself still sitting on the stage meditating.

"That's thirty minutes," Zack said.

Sophia opened her eyes, his voice jolting her out of meditation like a bucket of cold water suddenly drenching her while she slept.

Zack brought his thanatometer to eye level, looked at it, and smiled.

"It's kind of infuriating isn't it," he said, dropping his arm and looking at Sophia. "My PDA goes up when I imagine it doesn't exist but then it drops back down when I open my eyes and check out how much life I've gained."

"You shouldn't look," Sophia said, closing her eyes.

"How's yours?"

Sophia shrugged.

Zack tilted his head to see Sophia's PDA.

Sophia opened her eyes and watched a defeated expression take over his face. "Same?" she asked.

He nodded and said, "I thought it would go up one of these times. At least a little. What were you thinking about?"

"The usual. A bare arm. Nothing."

"Your birthday?"

"A little."

"I don't get it. It works for everyone but you."

Sophia placed a hand on Zack's. "It's okay," she said. "I can't control what happens. And I've stopped trying."

Zack gave a melancholic smile, stood up, and went into the kitchen. Sophia followed him with her eyes and then turned away to gaze out the window on the opposite side of the room.

He poured a glass of water and said, "I'm glad you came back."

"Me too," Sophia said, turning back to him.

"I didn't think I'd see you again."

He took a sip and walked the glass over to her. She took it, thanked him, and drank.

"You're much calmer now," Zack said.

Sophia laughed while drinking, almost sending water up and out her nose. She covered her mouth and swallowed, her eyes watering after she choked slightly.

She glared up at him playfully and said, "Thanks."

"What? I like it. I mean, you were fine before I just
—"

"I get it," she said chuckling and wiping her mouth.

Zack turned and disappeared into his bedroom. When he came back into the living room, he was carrying a small rectangular box. Sophia glanced at the box then up a Zack.

"Happy birthday," he said, resuming his seated position across from her and handing her the box.

Sophia took it and said, "But it's not for a couple of days."

"I know. I just wanted you to have it now. Open it."

Inside the box was a round stone, various shades of dark green with black spread throughout, two small purple candles, and a matchbook. Sophia picked up the smooth stone and felt somehow better with it touching her palm.

"It's a jade necklace," Zack said. "Jade's a protective and healing stone. It's also supposed to make you rich and fall in love but I got it for the protection and health. Money and love doesn't hurt though, right?"

"It's beautiful. Thank you."

"I thought you could wear it the day before your birthday. Apparently if you burn two purple candles for a bit with the jade stone between them, it makes it more powerful."

Zack spoke like an excited child about the stone, his face and arms animated. But after he had finished describing it to Sophia, sadness overcame his face and made it droop.

"I should go," Sophia said, putting the lid back on the box and standing up.

Zack stood and followed her to the door.

After slipping on her shoes, Sophia said, "Thanks for everything. The necklace, the meditation, helping me get the word out about my birthday."

"Me and everyone I know will be there. And everyone they know. And everyone they know. Don't worry."

"Right. Well, I'll see you there I guess."

They hugged, and Sophia left. As she walked down the hall to the stairwell, Zack stood in his doorway watching her leave. She turned, waved, and vanished down the stairs.

TWENTY-FIVE

Sophia stood in Rubin's living room, her thanatometer readout displayed on the large computer screen behind her:

PDA: 27

Age: 26.99

bpm: 60

Systolic: 120 mmHg

Diastolic: 80 mmHg

36.7 °C (98.1 °F)

23:55:37

"How do you feel?" Rubin asked, sitting in one of the only two chairs in his sparely furnished house, facing Sophia.

"Fine. A little nervous. But fine."

Two chairs, a lamp, a large Persian rug, the screen, and a vast cluttered bookshelf were the only things in his living room. The kitchen counters were bare and clean. There wasn't a dining table but rather two stools beneath an overhanging counter for eating. The two bedrooms had only beds, side tables, and lamps. The only things in the bathroom were towels, soap, and a bottle of 2-in-1 shampoo and conditioner.

Sophia enjoyed the simplicity of Rubin's house; it reminded her of her own apartment, which she hadn't been to since the day after she visited Skylark Haven, running in only briefly to grab some clothes and her tablet. Rubin thought it was safer to stay with him. And he was probably right, although Sophia hadn't heard anything about her grandfather's death since his memorial.

Rubin paid for everything, which was nice because the money her parents had given her was running out, and she wasn't going to ask them for more. She felt guilty about having them pay for a place she wasn't even living in anymore. She also felt guilty about freeloading off Rubin. She wished she could somehow repay the three of them for taking care of her, but there wasn't enough time.

"This is how it's going to feel," Rubin said. "Only instead of one person, whom you know, watching you, there'll be hundreds, maybe even thousands of strangers. All of them looking at you and your thanatometer readout."

"Are you going to get in trouble for this?"

"There's nothing illegal about what we're doing."

"Yeah but isn't your job to keep my PDA a secret? Won't helping me show it to as many people as possible get you fired? Or worse?"

"I stopped doing my job a long time ago. National Wellness wants you in a hospital room under quarantine. No," Rubin said, shaking his head. "What I was told to do doesn't really matter anymore."

At 12:02am, Rubin pointed at the screen and said, "There, you're twenty-seven and thousands of people are looking at you. How do you feel?"

Sophia turned to look at the screen. "I feel," she began, "the same." She turned back to Rubin. "I thought something would change twenty-four hours before but nope. Nothing's changed."

Rubin stood up and walked over to Sophia with a stylus in his hand. He took hold of her thanatometer, touched the display with the stylus a few times, and the screen behind Sophia went blank. "I'll have paramedics on standby tomorrow," he said quickly, examining her thanatometer. "Just in case."

"Are you sure you won't get in trouble for helping me?"

Rubin let go of Sophia's wrist, crossed his arms over his chest, looked into her eyes, and said, "It doesn't matter. This is what you have to do. People deserve to know."

"Thank you," Sophia said, putting her arms around Rubin.

Rubin uncrossed his arms and hugged her back.

"For everything."

"I didn't do—"

"Yes, you did. You did. Okay? So just say you're welcome and then shut up."

Rubin chuckled and said, "You're welcome."

Sophia squeezed him tight for a few seconds before letting go. Rubin also let his hands fall to his sides. He smiled an uneasy smile. Sophia smiled back before sitting down on the floor and looking at her thanatometer. She had less than twenty-four hours until she found out what she'd always been afraid and curious to know.

"Is everything ready for tomorrow?" she asked, looking up at Rubin.

Rubin nodded, sitting back down in his chair and turning off the screen with a remote. "It'll be just like a concert in the park. Only free and without the music," he said. "I've arranged for security to guard the area around the stage."

"What for?"

"Just in case. There's going to be a lot of people there. Anything could happen."

"You really think that many people will show up to see what happens?"

"They'll come. Out of fear, doubt, fascination, curiosity, faith."

"I hope you're right," she said, stretching out her legs in front of her and leaning back on her hands with her arms straight. "Do you think my parents will come?"

Rubin leaned forward, his forearms pressing into his thighs. "Have you talked to them?" he asked.

Sophia shook her head. "It's been almost a year," she said. "A year tomorrow since I've seen my mum."

"Are you going to call them?"

Sophia shook her head.

"Maybe they know already and will be there tomorrow night."

"Maybe," Sophia said, tracing the ornate designs in the carpet with her eyes.

"You should call."

"Not after what I did to my grandpa. I couldn't face them."

"You don't have to tell them about that."

"I won't lie to them either," she said, shifting to a cross-legged position, sitting hunched forward, picking at the carpet. "It's easier to just not see them."

She could picture her parents in their house at that very moment, her dad pacing across the living room, trying to act more angry than worried, and her mum looking to the door, unable to believe that the day had finally come, the day all other birthdays had been counting down to, the day she dreaded.

"Do you want me to call them?"

"No," Sophia said, looking up at Rubin, "you've done enough already."

Sophia stood up and moved across the living room towards the guest bedroom she'd been staying in for almost three months. "I'm going to bed," she said, walking past Rubin.

For a moment, Rubin watched speechlessly as she walked away. Then he called after her and said, "You changed everything you know."

She looked back over her shoulder at him.

"No matter what happens tomorrow. You changed everything when you were born," he said, standing and stepping towards her. "When I entered the nursery twenty-seven years ago, all the babies were screaming. I almost had to cover my ears they were crying so loud.

But when I found you, you weren't screaming. You lay there, in your incubator, sound asleep. Not crying, not fussing. And all the babies close to you weren't fussing either. There was a radius of calm around you. And standing beside you then I felt the same as I feel standing beside you now."

"How do you feel?"

"Like everything is going to be okay."

Sophia placed her hand in Rubin's and squeezed. He was such a kind man whose kindness she couldn't repay in a lifetime let alone in less than twenty-four hours. But there was something in his eyes that told her she, somehow, already had. That of the two of them *he* was the grateful one. Although she didn't understand it, she smiled, nodded in acknowledgement, and walked away. Even though she knew she wouldn't be able to sleep, she went to her room and shut the door.

Inside her room, Sophia took the purple candles out of the box Zack had given her and placed them on the bedside table with the jade necklace between them. Then she removed a match from the matchbook and lit the candles. As she watched the flames flicker, Rubin knocked on her door.

"Sophia."

"Yeah, come in," she said, facing the door.

Rubin opened the door and stood awkwardly in the doorway. He had a tiny metal cylinder in hand. He looked over at the candles without speaking.

"Is everything okay?" Sophia asked.

He turned to her. "Fine," he said. "I just have something to give you."

"You don't have to give me anything."

Rubin stepped forward and held out the cylinder. Sophia took it from him and examined it.

"What's it for?"

"There's something inside that I think you should have."

Sophia popped the cap off and then turned the cylinder upside down over her open palm. A thin disc fell into her hand; it had the same symbol on both sides: a circle with an arrow coming out of it.

"What is it?" Sophia asked without taking her eyes from the disc.

"It's a pregnancy disc," Rubin said. "Before couples needed to get permits to have children, they used one of those to find out on their own if the woman was pregnant or not.

"What does the symbol mean?"

"That one means the woman was pregnant with a boy. There was a different symbol for girls."

"Wow, it's cool," she said, looking up at Rubin. "But why are you giving it to me?"

"Because it was your mother's."

Sophia's mouth fell open. She looked back at the disc and cradled it in her palm.

"I know it's not my place to tell you this but you almost had a brother."

"I know," Sophia said, still staring at the disc. "My mum told me last year on my birthday."

Rubin sighed audibly, his breath shaky. "She did? Well, I'm glad that you know." He looked back through the open door and stepped towards it. "I'll let you get back to what you were doing."

"Wait," Sophia said, standing up. "Why do you have this?"

"Your mother didn't tell you that part?"

Sophia shook her head.

Rubin put his hand on the doorknob to steady himself. "I was the one that helped her," he said. "She made me promise to keep that. And even though I knew I should have incinerated it, I kept it. For her. For you."

"Thank you, Rubin," Sophia said, squeezing the disc in her hand.

"You're not angry with me?"

Sophia shook her head. Rubin smiled, and left the room, closing the door behind him.

Sophia placed the disc beside her necklace in between the burning candles. Then she lay in bed staring at the ceiling for a while before reaching for her tablet and checking her inbox for a message from her mother. There was one, and she opened it:

Lizette Nolan 12:01 AM (52 minutes ago)

Sophie,

> I sat outside your apartment today hoping I'd see you. But you never came home. I don't know where you are or what you're doing these days but I hope you're well. Please call or come see your father and me before your birthday. We both miss and love you tremendously.

Love always,

Mom and Dad

P.S. I have many regrets in life, not seeing or talking to you for the past year being the worst one. But I never once regretted having you as my daughter. I love you as you are for who you are. You've taught me more in twenty-seven years than I could have taught you in one hundred and twenty-seven. I'm sorry I wasn't there for

you more and that at times you suffered alone.
Please know, that in these final few hours, as in
every hour and minute and second of your life,
my heart and thoughts are with you. And they
will be with you always, my little Sophie.

Sophia wiped her watering eyes and clicked on the reply tab. She wrote to her mum to be at the park by 11:30pm tomorrow night and to come earlier if she wanted to be back stage for midnight.

TWENTY-SIX

Sitting in a chair, under the hot glare of lights suspended above her, in the middle of a large black stage with a gigantic screen hanging behind her and displaying her thanatometer readout, Sophia sat looking out at a never-ending sea of people. All eyes were on her and the screen behind her. She looked to the wings of the stage for Rubin and her parents, but no one was there. Then she searched the crowd for familiar faces but saw only one—Zack standing at the edge of the stage behind the row of security guards. She let her gaze linger on him and touched the jade stone hanging around her neck. It was almost eleven thirty on the eve of her twenty-seventh birthday.

The crowd wasn't loud, just a low rumble of subdued chatter.

Sweating, heart pounding, Sophia stood up and wiped her moist palms on her pants, thankful for the microphone hooked around her ear and dangling beside her mouth because she didn't think she would have been able to hold a mic.

"Thank you all for coming," she said, her voice, shaky and nervous, blasting through the speakers, too loud for her.

The murmur of the crowd subsided.

"It means a lot to me."

She sat down on the stage floor, crossed her legs, and rested her hands in her lap in dhyana mudra.

"I'm going to meditate until midnight," she said, looking out into the crowd, her voice calmer now that she was in her meditation pose. "Anyone who wants to join me is welcome to. I'll be imagining myself without a thanatometer and concentrating on the elation that comes with it."

Sophia sat up straight and sighed, her breath blowing into the mic, loud and powerful. She looked to the wings of the stage again and this time saw Rubin standing next to her mother; they were holding hands and smiling at her. Her mum waved. Sophia waved and smiled back. She wanted to run to her and hug her, not knowing if she were sensing her mum's desire or indulging her own. But she couldn't leave the stage, not with everyone watching her, not now that she'd started. There wasn't enough time. She checked the time on her thanatometer—11:31:15pm—returned her hand to her lap, faced the crowd again, and closed her eyes.

The bright stage lights pierced the darkness behind her eyelids. Whispers hissed through the crowd like a gigantic snake Sophia couldn't see. She thought of her mum and wondered where her dad was. She hated him for not coming but also understood. She felt hot beneath the lights and under the scrutiny of the crowd, as if her flesh was beginning to cook. Wanting to scream, she squeezed her eyes shut tighter. *What are they all thinking? Why are they here? It doesn't matter. It doesn't matter.* She inhaled and exhaled, her breath flowing through the speakers like wind in her ears, obscuring all other noises. *They're not here.* She inhaled and exhaled again. *Nobody is. Just me. No thanatometer. Just me.*

Just her breath and the darkness behind her eyelids. Then she sees herself sitting on the stage. Moving up and away from herself, like a camera zooming out, she sees the crowd; they move further and further away from her, receding until gone. Then the stage is gone and she sees herself as a white speck in a vast desert of darkness. Then she hears the crowd, a low hum at first as they begin to flow back towards her. She floats back down closer to herself, down, down, down, people's voices getting louder; the crowd moving in again. She hears her own breath and sees the backs of her eyelids. The crowd is loud now, cheering, calling out to her.

"Sophia! Sophia!"

She slowly opens her eyes—they feel heavy and weak. Countless people stand facing her, their mouths moving, an unintelligible jumble coming out. Only one voice is clear to her and it's calling her name—it's Zack's, he jumps up and down at the edge of the stage. Sophia makes eye contact with him; he stops jumping and points up behind her.

"Look!" he cries.

Sophia turns to the giant screen behind her:

PDA: 27

Age: 27

bpm: 56

Systolic: 120 mmHg

Diastolic: 80 mmHg

37.5 °C (99.5 °F) 12:01:37am

She checks her thanatometer and sees the same readout—she's twenty-seven and still alive. Sophia jumps to her feet. The crowd cheers, the powerful roar making her take a step back. She raises her arms; the crowd cheers louder. Lowering her arms, she notices that she can no longer feel her thanatometer. She looks down at it, still feeling nothing, and then begins to pull back the straps, using her teeth to help her. Her wrist starts to burn and throb, blood begins to trickle down her forearm, but she keeps pulling and prying the straps until the thanatometer is off her wrist and in her hand. The screen behind her goes blank. Her wrist feels cold as blood drips down onto the stage.

Sophia raises her bloodied wrist into the air, the thanatometer squeezed inside her fist. For a moment the crowd is subdued but then it erupts into cheers louder than before. Sophia drops the thanatometer and watches it hit the stage inaudibly. The throbbing worsens in her wrist. She regards her own blood and watches it drip down. Suddenly dizzy, she stands completely still for a moment.

"Sophie," Lizette yells from the wings.

She turns to her mum's voice, sees her and Rubin still standing there, and runs to them.

Standing in front of her mother at the side of the stage, she takes her hands in her own and says, "I didn't die. Can you believe it? I didn't die. I'm still here."

"I know, honey. I know," Lizette says frantically, tears running down her cheeks.

Lizette looks down at Sophia's bloody wrist and her face becomes stricken with concern.

"Oh, your poor wrist. Are you okay?"

"I'm perfect mum," Sophia says, throwing her arms around her mum and squeezing.

Blood smears across Lizette's back. Lizette kisses her daughter's cheek and squeezes back. Sophia then lets go of her mum, turns to Rubin, and hugs him.

With his arms around Sophia, he says, "Let me bandage your wrist," into her ear.

"No way," she says, leaning back and holding her bloody wrist up between them. "They have to see it."

Sophia turns back to the open stage, grabs Lizette's hand, and raises her crimson wrist over her head. Pulling Lizette out onstage with her, she walks to the front of the stage and jumps down between two security guards, turning back to help Lizette down.

Rubin rushes forward as Sophia and Lizette begin to make their way through the crowd. He calls out, but they don't hear him. He taps the closest security guard on the shoulder and says, "Follow them."

The security guard rallies other guards, but moving forward is difficult because the crowd is thick and swarming behind the two women. Rubin watches from the stage for a moment before jumping down into the crowd and trying to make his own way to Sophia.

With her mother squeezing her hand on one side of her and Zack beside her raised arm, Sophia moves forward through the crowd. Everyone moves aside for her. Some people reach out just to touch her, others embrace her—Sophia hugs back without letting go of her mother's hand, unintentionally smearing blood on backs before throwing her arm back up in the air— some keep their distance but still fall in step behind her. She sees thanatometers lying on the ground and many people helping each other to remove them. The ones who have taken off their thanatometers raise their bloody wrists into the air as they follow Sophia, flinging their thanatometers at the dark sky or twirling them around over their heads or simply letting them fall to the grass where they get pushed into the earth by marching feet. As Sophia moves through the crowd, her group of followers grows bigger and louder. She smiles and laughs and cheers with them.

Moving forward, a group of people emerges in front of Sophia. They don't move aside as she approaches; they stand still. Sophia tries to stop walking so she doesn't run into them but the momentum of the people behind her pushes her forward. A woman in front of Sophia yells something unintelligible before pushing her with both hands. Sophia stumbles back but is caught by those behind her. The woman yells again and the others with her shout things too, but the deafening roar of the crowd renders them voiceless. Zack and others rush forward; they push through the people blocking the way and make a path. Fighting breaks out in front of Sophia. She yells for them to stop, but nobody hears her. Lizette tries to pull Sophia back towards the stage but forward is the only way they can go. Sophia lets go of her mother's hand to break up a fight in front of her. She gets in between two combatants and pushes them apart. Others help her and some of the skirmishes are stayed but more rage on farther up ahead. Sophia hurries forward to get to the fighting, and a gunshot rips through the crowd, stopping it dead. As Sophia looks around to see where the shot came from, another rings out—she's hit in the side of the head, clutches her wound with both hands, and falls to the ground, blood pours onto the grass from beneath her hands.

Sophia is numb. She stares up at the people rushing around her, her mum kneeling down and wrapping her hands around her head, Zack pushing people back, others helping him hold the crowd at a distance. A circle forms around Sophia. She looks up at the sky and sees the few stars that haven't been extinguished by the city lights; she feels as if she can touch them. Rubin squats down in front of her, obscuring her view of the night sky. His mouth is saying her name but she can't hear him. She hears only a high-pitched ringing as she watches Rubin pull out his phone and talk into it. He drops the phone and removes his shirt, ripping it into strips that he ties around her head. For a moment Sophia feels the pressure of the thick, soggy fabric squeezing her head, the squeeze of Rubin's hand around hers. Then nothing. The ringing stops and all she can see is the dark dark sky.

TWENTY-SEVEN

Unconscious, Sophia lay wrapped in the sterile white sheets of a hospital bed, the multiple layers of hygienic gauze wrapped around her wound covering half of her face and making her head appear extremely swollen. The oxygen mask over her mouth and nose had a tube running to a respiratory machine beside the bed. Her right wrist, where her thanatometer had been, was also bandaged and a new thanatometer was fastened to her left wrist, a thick glowing cable attaching it to the computer housed in the bed frame.

Lizette sat beside the bed. She held Sophia's right hand between both of hers and stared up at her daughter's face. Sean stood in the corner farthest from Sophia, staring at the floor just in front of the bed, his arms crossed over his chest.

Inside an adjacent room, Rubin gazed through a two-way mirror at Sophia's closed right eye, one of the only visible parts of her face. Beside him, a computer screen displayed Sophia's thanatometer readout:

PDA: 27
Age: 27.00
bpm: 50
Systolic: 110 mmHg

Diastolic: 70 mmHg

37.0 °C (98.6 °F)

3:37:02pm

He could still hear the surgeon's voice in his head: *Bullet too deep. Lucky to be alive. May never regain consciousness.*

Rubin wished she'd wake up. He hoped for her eye to open and look around but somehow knew it never would again. Sophia was trapped—her mind a prison for the bullet, her body a prison for her mind.